A Minute's Silence

A Minute's Silence

by
Siegfried Lenz

translated from the German by
Anthea Bell

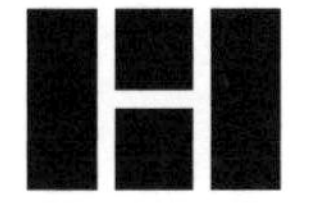

First published in Great Britain in 2009 by Haus Publishing Ltd,
70 Cadogan Place, London SW1X 9AH
www.hauspublishing.com

A CIP catalogue record for this book is available from the British Library

ISBN 978-1-906598-44-0

Typeset in Minion by MacGuru Ltd
Printed in Vicenza by Graphicom
Jacket Illustration: Detail of *Storm approaching from the sea* by Max Beckmann. Courtesy akg-images

For Ulla

"Here sit we down in tears and grief," sang our school choir at the beginning of the hour of remembrance. Then Herr Block, the principal, went over to the rostrum, which was surrounded by wreaths. He walked slowly, hardly glancing at the crowded school hall, and stopped in front of Stella's photograph on its wooden easel. He straightened up, or seemed to straighten up, and then bowed very low.

While he stayed in that position, Stella, in front of your photo, which had a black, ribbed silk ribbon running diagonally across it – a mourning ribbon in your memory – while he stood there bowing, I looked at your face. It wore the thoughtful smile so familiar to the oldest school students, that was us, from your English lessons. I looked at the short black hair I'd caressed, the bright eyes I'd kissed on the beach of Bird Island. I couldn't help thinking of that, and I remembered how you encouraged me to guess your age. Herr Block spoke to your photograph, looking down at it, he called you our much loved and highly esteemed Stella Petersen, he went on to say that you had been on the Lessing High School teaching staff for five years, that you were greatly valued by your colleagues and popular with the students. Nor did Herr Block forget to mention your commendable work on the School Textbooks Committee, and finally he reminded us that yours had been a cheerful nature: "Students who went on her school outings always spoke with enthusiasm, long after the event, of her good ideas, the mood she conjured up among all the young people, the sense of community they felt in studying at Lessing High School. That was what she created, a spirit of community."

A warning sound of shushing came from the front row by the windows where the little ones stood, the Grade Three kids who never stopped talking about their own affairs. They were pushing and shoving, they had something they wanted to show each other, their class teacher was trying to shut them up. You looked lovely in the photograph. I knew that green sweater, and the silk scarf with the pattern of anchors on it; you were wearing it back then on the beach of Bird Island where the stormy wind drove us ashore.

After the principal, one of the students was also to speak. They'd asked me first, probably because I was our class delegate, but I said no. I knew I wouldn't be able to cope with it, not after all that had happened. Since I had turned the offer down, Georg Bisanz was going to be the student speaker, and indeed he himself had asked to say a few words in memory of Frau Petersen. Georg had always been her favourite student, and took glowing reports home. I wonder what you would have thought, Stella, if you'd heard his account of our class outing: the time we went to that North Frisian island where the old lighthouse keeper told us about his work, and we waded in the shallows and got mud all over our legs. He mentioned the mud on your legs too, and how you held your skirt up, and felt more flat-fish with your bare feet than anyone else. Georg went on to talk about that evening at the Ferry House. When he said how good the fried flounders were, he spoke for all of us, and I knew just how he felt when he enthusiastically recalled the way the evening ended with sea shanties.

We all sang along that evening, we knew "My Bonnie Lies Over the Ocean" and "Off Madagascar As We Lay", and all the other sea songs. I drank two beers, and to my surprise Stella was drinking beer as well. Sometimes I felt that you were one of us, another student; you enjoyed the same things as we enjoyed, you were amused when someone put caps on the stuffed sea-birds standing around everywhere – paper caps, he folded them very cleverly. "And how pleased we were, my dear colleagues," said the principal to the staff, "when two students won scholarships to Oxford." To make the significance of his meaning crystal clear, he nodded to Stella's picture and repeated quietly, "Scholarships to Oxford." However, a sudden sob was heard, as if that statement could be understood differently. The man sobbing with his hand over his mouth was Herr Kugler, our art teacher. We'd often seen him and Stella walking the same way home together. Now and then she used to take his arm, and he was so much taller than Stella that it sometimes looked as if he were dragging her along. Several of the younger kids nudged each other and pointed out the weeping teacher. Two Grade Three pupils only just managed to suppress a giggle.

Herr Kugler hadn't been among the spectators when we were working on the breakwater. He'd been away on a yacht sailing in the Danish islands at the time. He was a tall, alarmingly thin man, and I'd certainly have noticed him among the onlookers that day. Most of them were summer visitors.

They came over the beach from the Seaview Hotel, many of them in swimsuits, climbed up on the pier and made their way all along as it went out to sea, right to the end of the pier, where they looked for a place to sit near the flashing light or on one of the mighty stone bastions. Our battered black barge, fitted out for carrying stones, was already lying just off the Hirtshafen entrance to the bay, secured by two anchors and loaded up to deck level with muddy, seaweed-covered rocks. We had dredged them up to widen and reinforce the breakwater and repair the pier, which had been damaged when winter storms knocked a number of stones out of its structure. A moderate nor'easterly wind promised a good spell of fine summer weather.

At a sign from my father, Frederik swung out the derrick boom, lowered the grab-bucket, positioned the metal teeth above one rock so that it was tightly gripped, and when the winch began turning and the colossal boulder rose jerkily from the hold, swaying gently back and forth over the side of the deck, the spectators stared spellbound. One of them raised his camera. My father gave another signal, the metal teeth of the grab-bucket opened, let the massive rock drop, and the water splashed up where it hit the surface, making waves boil and bubble in turbulence that took some time to die down.

I put on the diving mask and slipped over the side of the barge into the water, to check the position of the rocks, but I had to wait until the flurry of mud and sand had rolled away and settled in the light current. Only then could I see that the big rock we had just sunk was well placed. It lay across other rocks, leaving gaps and cracks between them, in line with our calculations, thus allowing water to drain away when the current washed around the breakwater. When my father cast me an inquiring glance I was able to reassure him. Everything was lying just as it should if we wanted to build the breakwater up. When I climbed back on board, Frederik offered me his packet of cigarettes and gave me a light.

Before he brought the grab-bucket down over the next rock, he pointed to our audience. "Hey, Christian, see that girl in the green swimsuit, the one with the beach bag? I reckon she knows you." I recognized her at once, her hairstyle and her broad-cheeked face immediately told me who she was, Stella Petersen, my English teacher at Lessing High School. "Do you know her?" asked Frederik.

"Yes, she's my English teacher," I said.

"What, her?" Frederik asked, incredulously. "Looks more like a schoolgirl herself."

"Don't let that fool you," I said. "She has to be some years older than us."

I'd recognized you at once, Stella, and I thought of our last conversation before the summer holidays, your warning and your encouragement. "Christian, if you want to make the grade you really ought to work a bit harder. Read *The Adventures of Huckleberry Finn*, read *Animal Farm*. We'll be looking at those books again after the summer break."

Frederik wanted to know how my teacher and I got on, and I said, "Well, could be better."

She was watching Frederik with interest as he brought his grab-bucket down over a huge black colossus, raised it in the air and let it hover for a moment over the now almost empty cargo space. However, he couldn't keep the rock from slipping out of those metal teeth and slamming down on the steel-lined bottom of the barge so hard that the whole boat shook. She called to us, she waved and gestured, indicating that she'd like to come aboard, and I pushed out the narrow gangplank, thrust it over the side, and found a flat stone at the foot of the pier where it could rest securely. Confidently, without a moment's hesitation, she came over to us, rocking on the balls of her feet a couple of times, or trying to, and then I reached out my hand and helped her on board. My father didn't seem too pleased to have this stranger visiting us. He moved slowly towards her, looking at me inquiringly, expectantly, and when I introduced her to him – "This is my English teacher, Frau Petersen" – he said, "Well, there's not much to see here." But then he shook hands with her and asked, smiling, "I hope Christian isn't giving you too much trouble?"

Before she replied, she looked searchingly at

me, as if not quite sure of her verdict on that point yet. However, then she said, in an almost indifferent tone, "Christian's doing fine."

My father just nodded; he hadn't expected any other answer. With his usual thirst for information, he immediately asked whether she had come for the beach party. The Hirtshafen beach party attracted a lot of people, he added, but Stella shook her head. She had friends who were sailing nearby in their yacht, she said, and they were going to pick her up in Hirtshafen in the next day or so.

"Yes, these are good sailing waters," said my father. "Yachtsmen think highly of them."

The first craft to pass the breakwater we'd been reinforcing that day was a small fishing cutter on her way home. She moved safely towards the harbour mouth, the fisherman throttled back his engine and came in beside us, and when my father asked what his catch was like he pointed to the flat boxes of cod and mackerel. A poor catch, just enough to pay for his diesel, not enough plaice, not enough eels, and off Bird Island a torpedo had tangled itself up in his net, he told us, a blank torpedo, the fishery protection vessel had taken it on board. He looked at our cargo of rocks, then at his catch, and said in friendly tones, "You're on to a good thing, Wilhelm, you just take what you need out of the water. Rocks stay put, you can always rely on rocks."

My father asked for some fish, saying he'd pay later, and added, turning to Stella, "No money changes hands in an open boat on the water, that's our custom." After the fisherman had cast off again, my father told Frederik to hand out mugs and pour us some tea. Stella accepted a mug of tea, but declined the shot of rum that Frederik was about to add. Frederik helped himself so generously that my father felt it incumbent on him to speak a word of warning.

Frederik raised the last rock of our cargo very slowly, swung the derrick boom over until the huge stone was moving just above the surface of the water, and lowered it where we were shoring up the breakwater. He let it down, he didn't allow the stone to drop but gently lowered it, and nodded, satisfied, when the water rose and broke above the big boulder.

You marvelled at the size of those mighty rocks, Stella, you asked how long they would have been lying on the seabed, how we found them, how we brought them up; you thought some of them looked like creatures that had been fossilized and so become immortal. "Does looking for them take long?"

"A stone-fisher can always tell where to go," I said. "My father knows whole stone-fields, and artificial reefs built a hundred years ago, and he goes searching for those. He carries the sea-chart showing the richest sources of big blocks around in his head."

"I'd like to see those stone-fields some time," said Stella.

A call came across the water to her; one of the Hirtshafen boys had pushed through the onlookers and was shouting. Since she didn't seem to have heard him, he dived off the pier and into the water. A few strokes brought him to the barge. He nimbly climbed the rope ladder. Ignoring the rest of us, he turned straight to Stella and gave her his message: it was something to do with a phone call, she was wanted on the phone in the hotel, she was to be there when the caller rang again. And as if to emphasize the importance of his errand, he added, "I'm to take you back."

It was Sven, the ever-cheerful Sven, a freckled lad and the best swimmer I knew. I wasn't surprised when he pointed to the hotel and the long wooden bridge, and said maybe Stella would swim back with him. Not just that: he suggested a race. Stella was so pleased that she gave him a hug, but she wasn't accepting Sven's challenge. "Some other time," she said. "We'll definitely have that race some other time."

Without asking her, I hauled in our inflatable dinghy, which was on a long line behind the barge, and she was ready for me to take her back to the wooden bridge at once.

Sven climbed into the inflatable after her, sat down beside her and put an arm around her shoulders in the most natural way in the world. The outboard motor chugged steadily, and Stella dipped one hand in the water during the crossing. She didn't mind when Sven scooped up a handful of water and let it run down her back.

I couldn't tie up to the bridge because all the moorings there were occupied by little Optimist class sailing dinghies. Their regatta would be one of the high points of the beach party. So we simply ran in on the beach and grounded our inflatable. Sven jumped out and went off to the hotel ahead of us, very full of himself, a messenger whose mission was successfully accomplished.

Waiters were carrying out chairs and tables, a drinks van was being manoeuvred into position under a windblown pine tree. Wires supported on poles were stretched right across the sandy beach, with coloured light bulbs dangling from them. A small mound had been raised for the band. Old men were sitting on navigation marks that had been hauled in to be given a coat of preservative; they didn't talk much, but cast an expert eye on the preparations for the beach party, probably thinking of parties of the past. None of them responded when I said hello.

Since Stella didn't come back, I went into the hotel.

A uniformed doorman at the entrance either couldn't or wouldn't tell me anything, except that Frau Petersen had made a phone call, and then gone to her room. She didn't want to be disturbed.

I went back on my own to the barge, where they were now waiting for me, and sent me down right away to check the way the stones were lying. There wasn't much to adjust. Now and then, but not often, I lowered the grab-bucket over a rock, signalling to Frederik which way to move it and where to bring it down again. Just once, when I suddenly had a blurred view of a huge boulder in the teeth of the grab-bucket over me, I got myself to safety fast, without giving a signal. This particular boulder didn't want to lie in its predestined place; my father had wanted it to rest on the breakwater like a kind of coping-stone, but instead it tipped sideways, turned right over, and did not reach the bottom but stuck fast between two dark rocks of the same size. Frederik and my father now inspected the results of their labours, and when one of them pointed to the beach and asked, "What do you think?" the other replied, "No, it won't be like the wind back then." He was referring to a beach party five years ago, when darkness unexpectedly fell over the beach, a squally wind blew in from the sea, playing havoc with the decorations, and the boats in the harbour basin were slammed against the pier.

I scanned the hotel and the beach café through Frederik's field-glasses, and I wasn't surprised to see people sitting at some of the tables already. Inside one window of the hotel building, which was painted pale green, I saw Stella, still in her swimsuit, talking on the phone. She talked, she perched on the window-seat and went on talking, meanwhile looking out at our bay in the still evening light, its water populated by seabirds drifting on the gentle swell.

Once she jumped up, took a few steps towards the window – her movements suggesting protest, disappointment – then returned to where she had been sitting, and I saw her holding the receiver at arm's length, as if to dissociate herself from whatever she was evidently being asked to do. Suddenly she put the receiver down, sat there thoughtfully for a while, then picked up a book and tried to read. As you sat there reading, Stella, I couldn't help thinking of one of those window pictures that invite the viewer to look beyond what the picture actually shows and indulge in speculation.

I kept the field-glasses trained on you, until Frederik nudged me and repeated what my father had just said: time to knock off work for today.

There had certainly been no plans for Herr

Kugler to speak during the hour of remembrance, but suddenly there he was in front of the rostrum, bowing to Stella's photograph and staring at her intently, as if that might conjure her up in person. He dabbed his face with a white handkerchief, he made little swallowing movements, and then he turned to you with a helpless gesture. "Why, Stella?" he asked. "Why did this have to happen?" I wasn't surprised to hear him call her by her first name and ask, in genuine distress, "Was there no other way out for you?" Neither our principal nor the other staff members present seemed to find the intimacy in his voice unexpected. Their faces still wore the bereft expression of mourning.

I found myself thinking involuntarily of our beach party, the three-man band trying to play cheerful, entertaining tunes, and I saw the Hirt-shafen locals coming down to the beach, hanging back a little but curious to see how the party would go.

They walked across the little park with its sparse trees, trudged through the sand on the beach, obviously wondering who would have come to the party and who had stayed away, and after some hesitant greetings they made their way to vacant tables and signed to the waiters. Orders were given for beer and apple juice, and shots of spirits at the table where three young men in sailors' jackets were sitting. I found a place next to an old man who was dozing as he stared into his beer glass while the frothy head slowly subsided. He was pleased when I confirmed that yes, I was indeed Wilhelm the stone-fisher's son – that was all he wanted to know. Suddenly I felt a hand on my back, heard a subdued giggle, the hand went on softly caressing me as if wondering when I would notice it. I turned swiftly, grabbed, and found that I had hold of our neighbours' little girl Sonja. She wriggled and squirmed, but I held tight and got her to calm down by admiring her dress, which had a pattern of ladybirds in flight, and the little daisy-chain wreath she was wearing on her head.

"Are you going to dance, Christian?" she asked.

"Maybe," I said.

"With me too?"

"Who else?" I said.

She confided that her father was going to come to the party with his eel-rake, the five-pronged one, so that people would think he was a sea-god with a trident.

When Stella appeared in the hotel doorway, and very slowly came down the few steps to the beach café, conversation died down at some of the tables, the men in sailors' jackets turned their heads – someone might have been pulling a string to work them – and as if Stella's appearance had given them their cue the band struck up *La Paloma*. I didn't need to wave to her; she came straight over to us, I fetched a chair and left her to get to know Sonja.

Sonja was sipping her fruit juice. When a bonfire was lit down on the beach, and some of her friends went to feed it with driftwood – the wood wasn't quite dry, so it crackled and spluttered and sometimes sent out a shower of sparks – she didn't stay there with us; she wanted to go and look at the fire and find twigs and bits of plywood for it.

"Your neighbour?" asked Stella.

"My little neighbour," I agreed. "Our fathers work together, they're both stone-fishers." I thought of Stella saying she'd like to see the underwater stone-fields, and I asked when we could go out to look at them together.

"Any time," she said, and we made a date for next Saturday.

The electric light bulbs went out, but came on again next minute, went out once more, and after a moment they were once again casting plenty of light on the place marked out for dancing. This lighting effect was a sign that it was time to try out the dance floor, where the sand had been rolled to make a flat, firm surface. And no sooner had the first two couples taken the floor than two thin little arms were flung around me, and Sonja whispered, close to my face, "Come on, Christian, you promised." She was a light weight, very agile, very eager to keep pace with me, catching up with little hops and skips now and then. Her small face was serious. When we danced past our own table she waved to Stella, and Stella watched us appreciatively. After that Sonja didn't want to go back to the table with me, but stayed on the dance floor alone, dancing by herself, and looking so relaxed and rapt as she danced that she won applause from some of the lads in sailors' jackets, who had come over from the merchant navy training centre on the neighbouring island. But it seemed that she wasn't satisfied with her own performance, either that or she thought she needed to learn more, because when I danced with Stella she crouched down and watched us very attentively. She seemed to be counting our steps, taking note of the way we turned and twirled on the dance floor, sometimes she jumped up and imitated a movement, or the way we separated and then came together again. Now she couldn't wait for my dance with Stella to be over; once or twice she showed her impatience by patting the ground with the flat of her hand or tracing a line in the air, telling us it was time to stop. But we, Stella and I, didn't move apart just yet, not until we realized that Sonja was in tears, and then we took her hands and led her back to our table, where Stella picked her up, sat her on her lap, and comforted her by promising to dance with her some time.

The band took a break, and at a word of command the men in sailors' jackets stood up and formed a line on the dance floor, to the accompaniment of a bo'sun's whistle. One of them uncoiled a rope so that everyone in the line could hold it. They stood still for a moment, then bent down, bowed to each other, and braced their legs apart to make it look as if they were putting all their strength into lifting a huge weight. Only when they sang could everyone see it was just pretence. The song was deep and rhythmic, with something forceful about it, it seemed to concentrate their powers and guide them, and instinctively you assumed that they were miming the hoisting of a sail, a heavy main-sail. After this interlude they mimed exhaustion, formed a circle and sang two well-known shanties, with our own Hirtshafen locals singing along. Waiters brought them beer donated by an anonymous patron.

As usual at every Hirtshafen beach party, the local sea-god known as the Kraken Man put in an appearance. Sonja's father came up from the water carrying his eel-rake, his shirt and trousers clinging to his body, a garland of seaweed round his neck. He was welcomed with applause and a show of great deference. When he jammed the five-pronged rake he had been carrying like a sceptre into the ground, children ran to their parents. He stared grimly at the company all around him, growling, and I knew he was looking for the girl he would choose as mermaid. Then he walked slowly from table to table, smiling, stroking and patting, assessing the girls, bowing apologetically when he decided against one of them. He passed our table at first, but on the dance floor he suddenly turned, seemed to freeze, struck his forehead, strode quickly back and bowed to Stella. Offering her his arm, he led her to the dance floor as if to display her, to show what a good choice he had made. And you happily played along, Stella: when he took you around the waist and twirled you, when he removed some of the seaweed from his neck and adorned you with it, when he drew your head down and kissed your forehead, you showed amusement and understanding for it all. Only when he was about to lead you down the beach and into the water did you resist, turning cheerfully back to Sonja, who ran to meet you and clung to you.

Sonja made Stella come back to our table, and after I'd ordered rum and cola and straight cola, Sonja asked something that seemed to be weighing on her mind: did Stella have a husband, and if so why wasn't he here? Was she really a teacher? I had said so when I was dancing with her, Sonja, she added. Was Stella a very strict teacher? Stella answered all her questions patiently, even when Sonja asked whether I would have to repeat a year at school for not working hard enough. She said, "Christian can do it – if he takes the trouble to try, he can do anything he likes." In reply to that, Sonja announced, "Christian is my boyfriend," and Stella stroked her hair with a gentle gesture that moved me.

When the band embarked on *Spanish Eyes*, some of the young men in sailors' jackets ventured on to the dance floor themselves, and a big fair-haired lad who had been turned down by the local girls came over to our table, walking unsteadily, sketched a bow, and asked Stella to dance. He was swaying, he had to hold on to the table top. Stella shook her head and said quietly, "Not today, thank you." At that the young man stood up very straight and inspected her with narrowed eyes, his lips quivering. An expression of hostility swiftly formed on his face. Then he said, "We're not good enough for you, is that right?" I was about to stand up, but he pushed me back, his heavy hand pressing on my shoulder. I looked at his bare toes, and was about to raise my foot when Stella jumped up and pointed to his friends, her arm outstretched. "Please go away now – look, they're waiting for you." That stopped the young man in his tracks. He puffed out his cheeks, but then moved away with a dismissive gesture. Stella sat down and sipped her drink, the glass shaking slightly in her hand. She smiled, she seemed surprised by the effect of her reproof, and perhaps amused by her successful performance. But suddenly she stood up, gave Sonja a swift goodbye caress, and made for the hotel entrance, knowing that I was following her. At reception, she asked for her room key. She did not explain anything.

All you said was, "I'm looking forward to Sunday, Christian."

The two boys who came into the hall late must have been among those who had to come to school by public transport; maybe they had missed their bus, maybe the bus had been delayed. Anyway, there they suddenly were at the doors of the hall: two ash-blond boys in clean shirts, both carrying bunches of short-stemmed flowers. They made their way forward very carefully. If they noticed a glance of disapproval, they put a finger to their lips or gestured apologetically. One of them was Ole Niehus, who had won the Optimist class dinghy regatta at our beach party. Ole was a friendly dumpling of a boy; no one would ever have expected him to win.

The put their flowers down in front of Stella's photo, made a little bow, and then walked backwards away from it to mingle with the members of the school choir, Ole looking as pleased with himself as if he had won another victory.

The way he climbed into his dinghy, it had looked as if he wouldn't even reach the starting line of the race. His plywood boat rocked and heeled over so far that it was almost shipping water. By comparison with the other young sailors, Ole had difficulty getting away from the wooden bridge to which they had all tied up. The wind had risen on the day of the regatta. Our *Katarina*, the old excursion boat that my father had said I could take out that day, was lying ready; the race umpires, three men in white, each with a pair of field-glasses dangling in front of his chest, came on board, and before we cast off Stella appeared on the bridge, Stella in her beach dress and wearing her green swimsuit under it. She asked me with a great show of formality whether she could watch the regatta from the *Katarina*, and I helped her up to the high seat behind the wheel. The armada of lightweight dinghies, yellow and brown and piratical black, sailed up to the starting line, the wind caught and rocked them, giving the young sailors some work to do. One of the umpires fired a flare, which went off before falling into the water. Flocks of seabirds rose in the air, screaming, flew around and then, still screaming, settled again. Sudden gusts of wind caught the sails. It wasn't easy for the sailors to keep on course for the buoy where they must turn, and sometimes the sails flapped so vigorously that a sound like the crack of a whip echoed over the water.

This was not a steady, regular, gliding progress, not a race in calm seas; the wind seemed to favour some of the dinghies more than others. For some competitors the race ended at the first buoy. One of these was Georg Bisanz, Stella's favourite pupil, who turned too close to the buoy and scraped it. His sail began flapping, his mast keeled over and the trough-shaped dinghy capsized – not dramatically, but curiously calmly, in a matter-of-fact way.

Georg emerged from under his sail, which was now lying flat on the water, he grabbed the mast and tried to hoist the sail back up by bracing himself against the hull of the dinghy, but he couldn't manage it. It was beyond him. I took the *Katarina* over to the scene of the accident; Stella placed her hand on mine where it held the wheel, as if she must help me. "Closer, Christian, we must get closer to him," she said, leaning towards me. Georg gave up the attempt to hoist his sail; he sank for a moment, re-surfaced, and threw both arms up in the air. One of the umpiring team took a red and white lifebelt out of its holder and flung it to him. The inflated ring fell on top of the sail and lay there sloshing about. In his attempt to reach it, Georg went under the sail again. Our *Katarina* was merely bobbing on the water with her engine turned off, while the umpires made various suggestions. In the end Stella decided to deal with matters in her own way. I remember how you took off your beach dress, Stella, hauled out the line from the cable drum in the stern, and handed me the end of it. "Here, Christian, tie me fast." She stood before me with her arms spread wide, a commanding look in her eyes. I slung the rope around her waist, pulled her body close, Stella placed both hands on my shoulders, and I was tempted to embrace her, I thought I could tell from her glance that she was expecting it, but one of the umpires shouted, "Come on, lower the ladder, we're off!" So I led you, hand in hand, to the rope ladder. You climbed straight down into the water, dived under, and then, as I paid out the line, swam over to Georg with a strong crawl. Stella resolutely freed herself from Georg as he came up again, clutching at her with both arms. He seemed to be trying to pull her down with him under the sail lying flat on the water, but she struck him smartly once on the throat and once on the back of his neck, and that was enough to make him loosen his grip. He let go of her. Stella grabbed him by the collar of his shirt and signalled to me, I hauled the line in, pulling strongly and steadily, and got them close enough to the ladder for us to heave Georg aboard. Stella swam back to his dinghy and fastened the line to a thwart, firmly enough for us to be able to tow the little craft.

The spokesman for the umpiring team – the bearded owner of the biggest marine equipment store on the coast, everyone in Hirtshafen knew him – expressed his appreciation to Stella, praising the way she had brought Georg to safety.

Over where the smaller kids were standing beside the wall with the windows, there was a slight disturbance. Herr Pienappel, our music teacher, moved out in front of the school choir and then, at a sign from Herr Block, stepped back again. Herr Block put his head on one side, closed his eyes for a moment, then let his glance move over the assembled students and, in a quiet voice, asked us all to observe a minute's silence in memory of our dear Frau Petersen, who would never be forgotten. Lowering my head, I stared at your photograph, Stella. Most of the others bowed their heads too. There had never before been such a silence in our school hall as the one that now descended on almost everyone. And in that silence I seemed to hear the sound of oars.

Since the outboard motor of our inflatable was out of action, we took our rowing boat to the underwater stone-field. Stella insisted on taking the oars. How regularly she pulled them through the water; she was barefoot, bracing herself against a plank on the bottom of the boat, her smooth thighs slightly sun-tanned. I steered her past Bird Island, amazed by her stamina, and admired her as she lay far back and raised the oar-blades from the water. Just as we passed Bird Island a strong gust of wind caught us. She parried it skilfully, but couldn't keep the boat from being flung back towards the beach, where it ran aground, jammed against the stump of a root.

We couldn't free ourselves; even when I tried to pole the boat away with one of the oars, we were still stuck. We had to climb out. The water was knee-high as we waded to the beach, Stella holding her beach bag above her head. She was laughing; she seemed to find our misadventure funny. You were always ready to laugh. Even during lessons, certain mistakes amused her. She would discuss them, pointing out the comic or sometimes disastrous consequences that could result from mistakes in translation. The wind was getting stronger, and it was beginning to rain.

"Now what, Christian?" she asked.

"Let's ..."

"Another time," she said. "We'll go out to the stone-field some other time."

I knew the hut with its corrugated iron roof hidden among the reeds; it was used by the old bird warden who had spent many summers here. The door was hanging off its hinges, a pan and an aluminium mug stood on the iron stove, and the bedstead roughly cobbled together from bits of wood had a seagrass mattress on it. Stella sat down on the mattress, lit herself a cigarette, and examined the interior of the hut: the cupboard, the wooden table with its many notches, the mended gumboots hanging on the wall. What she saw seemed to amuse her. "Do you think we'll ever be found here?" she said.

"Oh yes, that's for sure," I said. "They'll come looking for us, they'll see the rowing boat and take us home in the *Katarina*."

It was raining harder now, raindrops drumming down on the corrugated iron roof, and I collected some odds and ends of wood left lying around and lit a fire in the stove. Stella was humming quietly, a tune I didn't know; she was humming it to herself as if absent-mindedly, or at least not for me to hear her. Lightning, still far away, flashed above the sea. I keep peering out, hoping to see the lights of the *Katarina*, but there was no sign of anything in the murky gloom above the water. I scooped rainwater out of a water-butt standing outside the hut, put the old kettle on the stove, and made camomile tea; I'd found a packet in the cupboard. Before handing Stella the aluminium mug, I drank a little myself. You took the mug, smiling. How beautiful you were as you raised your face, so close to me. As I couldn't think of anything else, I said in English, "Tea for two", and you replied, in the kindly tone I knew so well, "Oh, Christian."

Stella offered me a cigarette, and patted the bedstead beside her, inviting me to sit down. I sat beside her. I put a hand on her shoulder and felt that I longed to say something to her, yet at the same time all I wanted was for that moment to last, the moment when I was touching her, and that wish kept me from telling her what I was feeling. But then I remembered the book she had recommended me to read in the summer holidays, and I found it easy enough to mention *Animal Farm* and ask her why she had set us that particular book. "Oh, Christian," she said again, with her understanding smile. "It would be a good idea if you found that out for yourself."

I was on the point of apologizing for my question, because I realized that by asking it I had made her my teacher again; I had recognized her authority in the classroom at school, but here my question carried a different weight, and my hand on her shoulder also held a meaning that it wouldn't have had elsewhere. Here, Stella could understand my touch as merely a wish to reassure and calm her, and she did not object when my hand moved gently over her back. But suddenly she threw her head back and looked at me in surprise, as if she had unexpectedly felt, or discovered, something that she hadn't been reckoning with.

You leaned your head against my shoulder. I dared not move, I let you take my hand and lift it to your cheek, and you left it there for a moment. How different Stella's voice sounded when she suddenly stood up and went out to the beach. Once there, she made an attempt to right our rowing boat, which was lying on its side, but she couldn't shift it. Then, after a moment's thought, she picked up the tin can that always lay ready and began baling out water. She scooped up water so busily that she didn't notice the light approaching the beach: the bow light of our *Katarina*. It was Frederik and not my father at the wheel. He brought the *Katarina* in close enough to the shore for us to wade out, and he helped us on board. He didn't say much, he just remarked, when I put my windcheater around Stella's shoulders, "Good idea, that'll help."

No blame, no expression of relief at finding us. He nodded in silence when Stella asked to be taken to the bridge outside the Seaview Hotel, and he didn't even ask whether I wanted to go home or be dropped off at the bridge as well.

Stella didn't ask me to accompany her, she simply assumed that I would, and she did the same in the hotel, where there was no one at reception. Unhesitatingly, she took her key from the almost empty keyboard, nodded to me, and walked ahead of me to the stairs and then down the corridor to her room, which was on the side of the hotel facing the sea.

I sat down by the window and looked out into the twilight while she changed in the bathroom, switching on the radio as she did so and humming along with Ray Charles. When she came out again she was wearing a pale blue roll neck pullover. She came straight over to me, passed her hand over my hair, and then leaned down and tried to meet my eyes. Our *Katarina* was out of sight now. You said, "The boat will be on her way home, won't she?"

"It's not so very far to our place," I said.

"But won't they wonder where you are?" she asked, concerned.

"Frederik will tell them what they want to know," I said. "He works for my father."

She smiled, probably feeling that her concern was out of place, or even insulting because it reminded me of my age. She dropped a kiss on my cheek and offered me a cigarette. I said what a nice room it was, and she agreed, adding only that the bedspread seemed too heavy, she thought she'd have difficulty breathing easily at night. She picked up part of the bedspread for a moment, and as she did so a little glowing ash fell on the sheet, whereupon she let out a little cry of alarm and covered the burnt place with the palm of her hand. "My God," she whispered, "oh, my God." She pointed to the little black-rimmed mark, and as she repeated her cry of dismay I put my arms around her and drew her close.

She wasn't surprised, she didn't stiffen, there was a dreamy expression in her bright eyes, perhaps it was partly exhaustion, but you brought your face close to mine, Stella, and I kissed you. I felt her breath coming a little faster, I felt the touch of her breasts, I kissed her again, and now she released herself from my arms and, without a word, moved towards the bed. She didn't want to lay her head in the middle of the pillow, a long one with a flowered-patterned pillow case and room enough for two on it. With a deliberate movement she moved her head to leave half the pillow free, with plenty of space for me. Without a sign, without a word from her, but that pillow showed me clearly what she was expecting.

You could tell from the faces in our school hall that some of the students were better than others at observing the obligatory minute's silence. Most of them tried to make eye contact with their neighbours, some shifted from foot to foot on the spot, one boy was examining his face in a pocket mirror, and I saw another who had apparently succeeded in dropping off to sleep on his feet. Another was looking at his watch now and then. The longer the silence lasted, the more obvious it was that several students were finding it tough going to stand there and get through the time without drawing attention to themselves. I looked at your photograph, Stella, and I imagined how you would react, if you could, to the minute's silence in your memory.

We didn't leave a double imprint on the pillow; once our faces turned to each other, they came so close that only a single large imprint was left. By the time I stood up again Stella was asleep, or at least I thought so. I carefully took her arm, which was lying relaxed on my chest, and moved it to the bedspread. She sighed, she just raised her head a little way and looked at me, smiling, questioning.

I said, "I must go now."

"How late is it?" she asked.

I didn't know. I just said, "It's getting light. They're probably expecting me home." At the door, I stopped. I thought something ought to be said, a goodbye, or some reference to what lay ahead of us at school, in our separate everyday lives. I kept quiet, because I wanted to avoid saying anything that sounded final, or that Stella might understand as final. I didn't want what had begun so unexpectedly to come to an end. As if of its own nature, it demanded to go on longer.

When I opened the door she got off the bed, came over to me barefoot, put her arms around me and held me close.

"We'll see each other again," I said. "Soon." She did not reply, and I repeated it. "We have to see each other again, Stella."

I had never called her by her first name before, but she didn't seem surprised; she accepted it perfectly naturally, and as if to let me know that she was happy with that she said, "I don't know, Christian. You and I must both think what's best for us."

"But surely we can see each other again."

"We will," she said. "We're bound to, but it can't be the same as before."

I wanted to say: I love you, Stella! But I didn't, because at that moment I couldn't help thinking of a film starring Richard Burton, and he used exactly those over-familiar words saying goodbye to Liz Taylor. I caressed her cheeks, and I could tell from the expression on her face that she wasn't prepared to agree to my suggestion, or didn't feel she was in any position to do so. I buttoned up my shirt, put on my windcheater, which Stella had hung over the back of a chair, and said – even out in the corridor I realized what a poor sort of goodbye it was – “Well, I can always knock on your door at home, can’t I?”

I didn’t walk down the stairs, I leaped down them, full of a sensation I had never known before. There was someone at the reception desk now. When the man looked at me in surprise, I wished him “Good morning,” perhaps rather too cheerfully, for he did not respond and just stared thoughtfully after me as I went down to the beach. A fishing cutter was on her way out to sea, to the sound of the loud chugging of a diesel engine and surrounded by herring gulls. The water was calm. I went to the place where the navigation marks had been brought in and were waiting to be cleaned and painted, sat down, and looked back at the hotel. I immediately saw Stella at the window of her room. She waved. It seemed to be a weary wave; once she reached her arms out as if to catch me in them, and then she disappeared. Probably someone at the hotel entrance was asking for her.

Gernot Balzer, in my class and our ace gymnast, brilliant at floor exercises, nudged me and drew my attention to Herr Kugler, who was no longer sobbing but was now rubbing his throat and neck with a red and blue check handkerchief. Kugler, probably the most absent-minded art teacher ever on the staff of any school, then inspected his handkerchief as thoroughly as if there were something interesting to be discovered there. Gernot whispered to me, "I saw them, him and Frau Petersen," and went on to tell me, still in a whisper, what he had seen on the beach near the three pine trees. They both lay down in their swimsuits, he said, they were both reading. Gernot had an idea that he was reading something aloud to her, and I felt sure it was a chapter from the book on Kokoschka he was writing. He'd already told us about some of its main points. When a painter sees something, he had told us, he makes it his own. Absent-minded as he often was at school, he was bringing up his four children to a methodical plan. I once saw Kugler, whose wife was dead, in the dining-room of the Seaview Hotel with the four kids. They had hardly sat down at a table before he was ordering fish quenelles and apple juice for everyone, along with the paper and coloured crayons that were always on hand at the hotel to amuse tourists' impatient children. Before they began eating he told them to draw a vase, not its outline seen from the side but from above, looking into the opening at the top. I couldn't get my mind around the idea that he too might once have shared a pillow with Stella.

I wonder what he thought me capable of, or indeed just what he was after when he turned up at our place one Sunday morning? I'd been cleaning out the barge and was in the boathouse checking up on the ropes when I heard Herr Kugler's voice. He was talking to my father, who sounded none too friendly as he answered questions. Very likely he only answered them at all because Herr Kugler had introduced himself as my teacher. He had noticed, he said, that the rocks we had dumped between the boathouse and the beach were reminiscent of strange creatures. What he claimed to see in them said a lot for his powers of imagination. He thought he had seen one rock like a tadpole, others like a penguin, a monstrous egg, even a Buddha. My father listened to him patiently, laughed now and then, and kept any thoughts of his own to himself.

Herr Kugler was not surprised when I came out of the boathouse. He said he'd thought he'd like to take a look around our place here, that was all, but the way he stared at me, a cold, appraising assessment, made me doubt it.

The longer I studied your photo, Stella, the more it mysteriously seemed to come alive. Sometimes I thought you were giving me a look of silent understanding, just as I'd expected you would in the first English lesson after the summer holidays. You see, I'd been expecting us to communicate in secret ways that no one else in the class would notice. When you came into the room and we stood up, I suppose I was feeling more on edge than anyone else. "Good morning, Mrs Petersen." I felt restless. Stella had a white blouse on, a tartan skirt, and the necklace she so often wore, a thin gold chain with a little gold seahorse hanging from it. I tried to meet her eyes, but she took no notice, and the glance she gave me was almost indifferent. I wasn't surprised that right at the beginning of the lesson she encouraged us to tell her about where we had spent the holidays, and anything special that we had noticed – she'd done the same thing last year. "Try to express yourselves in English," she told us in that language. As no one volunteered, she asked Georg Bisanz, her favourite pupil, to start the ball rolling, and he was happy to launch into an account of his summer holidays, describing the armada of Optimist class sailing dinghies casting off from the bridge to race for the Hirtshafen Cup, and mentioning his "accident". Stella suggested "misfortune" as the right word for it. While Georg was still speaking, I sought for words I could put together to describe my own most interesting experience in the holidays, but I wasn't called upon. Stella didn't say anything like, "But now we'll listen to Christian." Georg's account was enough to satisfy her, and she went on to ask what we had found out about the life of George Orwell, whose novel *Animal Farm* we were going to study next. I was determined not to put my hand up. I looked at her legs, felt her slender body lying next to me again, the body I had embraced, I couldn't forget what had happened. I wanted the memory we shared to be confirmed by a gesture, a glance; close to her as I was, I didn't want to be alone with my memory. She did not seem surprised when I spoke up, but asked, "Yes, Christian?" So I told the class what I had found out about the author: his time with the police in Burma, his resignation in protest against certain governmental measures, his years living in poverty in London and Paris. As she listened to the information I had just acquired there was a strange brightness in her eyes, a gleam of recognition or involuntary memory, I thought I saw not just approval but also understanding there, and when she came over to where I was sitting and stood in front of my table I was expecting her to put a hand on my shoulder – her hand on my shoulder! – but she didn't; she didn't venture to touch me. However, I imagined her touch, and I also imagined myself standing up and kissing her, to the amazement of our whole class, and maybe not just them, I thought it possible that some of the young men who, I knew, had girlfriends, would react with a knowing smile or even applause. In my own class I'd have had to content myself with arousing curiosity.

Even after the lesson, out in the corridor, you

didn't look up as you passed me. I thought I sensed your displeasure with me for trying to attract attention by standing out from the other students. It may have been her turn to supervise break, but anyway, she sat on the green bench in the school yard by herself, lost in thought, or a least taking no notice of the smaller kids playing catch and scuffling the whole time.

Just as the school choir was about to sing again, a barrel organ started up out in the street. The small kids standing by the open windows couldn't help looking down immediately at the man turning the barrel organ and his instrument itself, they pushed and nudged each other, and some of them waved to the man, who was playing the tune of "Wooden Heart": *Can't you see, I love you? Please don't break my heart in two.* Herr Kugler nodded to me; it was a request to follow him out into the corridor, downstairs and outside. The organ-grinder, a small man with inflamed eyes, was standing under a chestnut tree. He couldn't understand why Herr Kugler was asking him to take his barrel-organ somewhere else, pointing to a side street leading down to the river, and even when Herr Kugler explained that he and his organ-grinding were disturbing a solemn hour of remembrance he was unwilling go away. He said he had tunes for all occasions in his mixed repertory, including some lovely sad pieces. Herr Kugler ignored this hint, saying, "Just please go away," and put a two-mark piece into the little tin dish standing on the instrument. The man didn't thank him, but moved slowly towards the low wall running around our school yard, sat down on it and smoked.

I was the one who threw the first coin on the "Round Bird Island" excursion. I was steering our *Katarina,* with holidaymakers from the Seaview Hotel on board, and a few lads from the Hirtshafen gang, barefoot and wearing only bathing trunks. She was on board as well, Stella, sitting on the seat in the stern looking relaxed and beautiful. When she climbed in we had merely grasped each other's hands for a moment. Sonja was sitting beside Stella, looking at her admiringly and fingering her gold bracelet. I didn't have to untie the *Katarina* myself; the lads who had begged to come on the trip were ready to help out, and showed their skill when, at my signal, they cast off both ropes. The mist had risen and dispersed long ago, the surface of the sea was glittering faintly, and where the sun reached the sandy bottom, left in a rippling pattern by the movement of waves now gone, it shone yellowish brown. We turned away, and some of the older passengers waved back to the beach, waving at random to the hotel waiters and the customers in the café. Sonja watched our wake running away at the stern. When I asked Stella to take the wheel she happily agreed. I enjoyed standing on the raised platform there beside her, and as if I wanted to correct our course I reached my hand out to the wheel and placed it on hers, feeling her responding to my gentle pressure. Quietly, so that only I could hear, she said in English, "As you see, Christian, I'm a sea-captain in training." And what she didn't yet know, she said, she'd soon learn when she spent a few days on board her friends' yacht.

We went around Bird Island, I slackened speed, and now we were gently gliding towards the mighty stone reef that went right down into the depths underwater, and was lost from view in the dark. Some of the tourists were hanging over the side of the *Katarina*, staring down and marvelling, telling other people what they could see. Finally they turned to me and asked the usual questions. They could hardly believe that the reef was artificial, built several hundred years ago by the primitive means then available; people had brought the boulders to this spot, methodically lowered them and piled them up, not high enough to show above the water but so that they were hidden just under the surface, a trap waiting for the keel of any unsuspecting ship coming in.

"So now anyone who wants rocks can come and help themselves," Stella said.

We gently skirted the reef, and when the sandy

promontory came into view a flock of water-fowl, mostly herring gulls, rose in the air like a white snowstorm. They flapped their wings, they screeched, and for several of the boys in the boat that was the signal they were waiting for. They'd intended to reach our present position from the first. The boys went to the side of the boat, circled their arms in the air and dangled their legs above the water. They all looked at us. The boat lay still now, the water was clear. I threw just one coin at first, and even before it reached the bottom, which was visible in the clear water, two of the boys were jumping in and diving towards it, swiftly dog-paddling or swimming to the bottom, and as usual I was fascinated to see their bodies twist and turn, sometimes moving as if in a dance. I threw two more coins in and encouraged the passengers to search their pockets and do the same. Some of them threw coins farther out, others let them drop close to the boat, waiting to see which boy would find and seize it, and if he would manage to keep it after a brief skirmish with the others on the sea bed. Their soundless tussling, accompanied by rising air bubbles, usually ended with the victor putting the coin between his teeth, swimming quickly in and coming on board up the short rope ladder that I had hung over the side. Grey-faced and breathless, they would drop on the nearest seat, and only now did the little divers look to see what their prize was, balancing it on the palm of a hand, showing it to the others.

I hadn't noticed Sonja jumping in at the same time as the boys, but then I saw her on the bottom, trying to defend herself against a rival diver who was clutching her and trying to open her hand by force. I was just thinking of taking the boathook out of its holder, to push Sonja's adversary away from her with the blunt end, when Stella stripped off her beach dress, tossed it to me, and jumped over the side, body stretched full length. A few strokes brought her down to the two children at the bottom, and she was forcing them apart by pushing the palm of her hand into the boy's face. She put an arm around Sonja and brought her to the rope ladder, but dived down again to retrieve the coin that the little girl had lost at the last moment. Then she climbed back on board, watched with approval by the passengers, and sat down beside Sonja, who was doubled up and breathing heavily, and didn't seem much gratified by the return of the coin. But her face brightened when Stella held her close, stroked her cheek, put one of her feet beside one of Sonja's and said, with amusement, "Look, we both have webbed feet!" Then she reminded Sonja that every home-coming from a trip around Bird Island had to end with a swimming race. The boys were already preparing to jump in, and as we passed the bridge outside the hotel I gave the word. They all went into the water and swam ashore, each in his own style. Some were doing dog-paddle, some the crawl, some forged swiftly ahead, many dived down for a moment and tried to swim faster under the water, many impeded their faster neighbours by clutching their legs or getting on their backs. Sonja was lost from sight in the spray and air bubbles thrown up by the contenders.

Stella wouldn't take part in this race. When I encouraged her to join in, she simply said, "It wouldn't be fair, Christian." At the time I didn't know that she'd swum in some kind of championships, I guess they were university championships, and had been in the medley relay team that came second.

Anyway, Stella, I wasn't satisfied with the reason you gave, and I told you so again when we were lying under the pine trees that warm, windless afternoon. We lay side by side, only in our swimming things, and I was stroking your back. I asked why she wouldn't join in the race, and she said, "That's easy to answer, Christian. I knew I mustn't win. If you're so much better than the others you mustn't compete. It would be unfair, a cheap sort of victory."

I didn't agree, I thought the reason she gave

was patronizing, even arrogant. I said, "But being better is something you've achieved for yourself. It's an honest ability."

She smiled and said, sighing, "Oh, Christian, you need the right conditions if you're going to get a result that means anything. The conditions have to be right." She kissed me, a hasty kiss, then she jumped up and ran lightly down to the water. "Come on, come in with me."

Swimming fast, twisting and turning, we made for deeper water, reaching out for each other. I drew her to me, pressed close to her body and held her. That amazement, I'll never forget that amazed look and that happy consent in it. Our bodies pressed against each other as if they'd been waiting for this. We laughed when the buoyancy of the water made it hard for us to stand there. I pointed to the two red flags blowing in the breeze – just scraps of fabric – warning swimmers of an eel-trap at that spot, and called, "Come on, Stella, once round the flags and the winner can make a wish." And without waiting for her to agree I swam away. At first I didn't look to see if she was following, I was swimming as fast as I could, the flags were bobbing in the moderate swell, I hadn't quite reached them when I glanced behind me for the first time. Stella had accepted my invitation, taken up my challenge, she was joining in, she was following me, doing long strokes in crawl. I thought she was taking it easy as she swam, sure of her victory, and that spurred me on. On reaching the flags she changed style and now, as if in high spirits, she was doing back-stroke without decreasing the distance between us. I put on a spurt, or what I thought was a spurt, and drew away by several metres, by now almost sure of reaching the beach ahead of her, but then she raised one arm and waved. It was the kind of wave someone sure of doing better would give, cheerful, forbearing, and she accelerated and swiftly caught up, her legs kicking and whirling, I felt as if she were being driven on by a ship's propeller. You passed me so easily, Stella! I didn't even try to catch up with you, I gave up, let myself drop back and watched as you waded ashore without the slightest sign of exhaustion.

Among the pines, in the hollow among the pines, I reminded her that she could make a wish. She declined; not now, she said, not at that moment, she'd come back to it some other time. It was always useful, she added, to have a wish available, and you had to think carefully about the right time to make it, you mustn't waste it. As she spoke she was brushing sand off my back and my chest, she once bent down so close that I thought she'd discovered something there, an old injury, a scar, but it was something else that had struck her. "It really does smile," she said, "your skin is actually smiling, Christian." Stella had once read that at certain moments the skin can smile, and now, it seemed, she'd found confirmation of the fact. Curious, and more than curious, I turned over on my side, but all I could see was that it was my skin, just as it always had been, and it didn't show so much as the suggestion of a smile. But what I couldn't see, or perhaps couldn't perceive, she could. Her remark had set off in me something that I wasn't prepared for: a restless longing that, in my imagination, began growing more and more urgent, made me touch her, I stroked her thighs and sought her eyes at the same time, our faces were so close that I could feel her breath. Her gaze held mine, I had a feeling that it responded to my longing, or that it was offering a gentle invitation. I took off her swimsuit, and she let me, she helped me, and we made love there in the hollow among the pines.

How ready she was to talk, as if now we had to say something that we hadn't yet said. The past came back into our minds, we wanted to know more about each other, for the sake of security or justification, or just to soothe us. Our need for that meant that we shrank from no questions. It's a long story, she said, as my head lay in the crook of her arm, and she said again, "It's a long story, Christian, it begins back during the war, in Kent, in the skies above Kent."

"How do you mean, in the skies?" I asked.

"My father was radio operator in a bomber, his plane was shot down on its first raid, his companions died in the crash but he survived, his parachute was working, so that's how I became an English teacher," she said.

"That's how you became an English teacher?" I asked.

And Stella told me about her father, how after being shot down he was taken to a POW camp near Leeds, where he spent some weeks giving himself up to apathy, like most of the prisoners. That changed when he and some of the others were sent to work on the land at harvest time. He enjoyed working on Howard Wilson's farm, and most of the POW agricultural labourers used the political lectures delivered to them back at the camp to catch up on their sleep. Stella's father ate at the same table as the Wilsons, he went to a modest birthday party they gave, and once they asked him to take their sick boy to a doctor in a trailer attached to a bicycle.

"Is your father a countryman himself?" I asked.

"He was an electrician," she said, "he could show people that there wasn't enough light in their houses, and prove it. Wherever he went he always had a couple of spare electric bulbs in his case. He'd leave them with his customers at cost price, and as a result his favourite customer called him Joseph the bringer of light. The Wilsons just called him Joe. He didn't tell us why one day, long after the end of the war, he decided to visit the Wilsons, he simply said it was about time to go and see them." Today, she said, she knew that it was very understandable to want to go back to a place where you'd had an important, maybe even crucial experience in the past. Then, after a pause, Stella added, "We were there for seven days, Christian, we were only planning to spend an afternoon with the Wilsons, but we stayed seven days."

I couldn't, I just could not take my eyes off her picture; while the school orchestra was playing I kept gazing at the photograph. It was as if we had made a date for this hour of remembrance in the hall, meaning to say something we didn't yet know about each other. I had heard our orchestra rehearsing twice, the orchestra and the choir, and now, in front of your picture, the Bach cantata unexpectedly took a strong hold on me. That sense of abandonment, that desperate search, the hope for an answer, for salvation, an appeal to the victorious power of the Father and the Son. God's time is the very best time, in the words of the cantata. How your face suddenly shone, Stella, the face I'd kissed all over, on your forehead, on your cheeks, on your mouth. Praise and glory unto the Lord, I call upon Thy names, I am resigned, glory unto

Thee. And then that Amen, taken up like an echo by our orchestra, an echo dying away, growing quieter and quieter, losing itself most wonderfully in a universe of consolation, the *Actus Tragicus* overcome. I stared at your face, I had never before felt a loss so powerfully – which was strange enough, because I had never before known what it was to have possessed what was lost.

When Herr Block stepped up on the rostrum, I thought he was going to make another speech, but he only thanked us for remembering her in silence. He did not actually ask us to leave the hall; without a word, he indicated the two exits, and the crowd began to move, became a traffic jam, thinned out, made for the corridors where voices immediately rose. I held back, I waited until the little kids had also found their way from the window wall to the exit, then I went up to the rostrum, looked briefly around me, and quickly snatched up Stella's photograph. I put it under my pullover and left the hall with the others.

There were no lessons after the hour of remembrance. I went downstairs to my classroom on the first floor, entered the empty room and sat down at my table. I put Stella's photograph in front of me. I couldn't sit like that for long; I put the photograph away in the drawer and decided to take it home and keep it beside the photograph of my class. A tourist had taken the class photo, an old retired teacher who was staying at the Seaview Hotel and knew Stella. He grouped us in his own way: the first row reclining on the ground, the second kneeling, the tallest students standing behind them, and in the background three fishing cutters putting out to sea in line. You were standing among the kneeling students, Stella, placing a hand on the heads of those closest to you. To one side of the picture – I don't know why – stood Georg Bisanz, Stella's favourite student, clutching a package to his chest with both hands: a package of exercise books, mine among them. It was Georg's privilege to collect the exercise books.

I wasn't surprised when, at the beginning of the double English lesson, she gave us the subject for the essay. Stella had told us ahead of time to read, among other books, *Animal Farm*, and I was merely disappointed by her cool, objective tone. There was no trace in her expression now of secret understanding, she did not indicate in any way what we shared and what was ours. She looked at me just as she looked at the others, even when she was standing beside my table – her body so close that I could have pulled it towards me – I thought I sensed an unexpected distance in her: what happened, happened, that's all, you can't call on it now.

I was sure I'd written that latest English essay

to Stella's satisfaction, I had enjoyed describing the animals' revolution on Mr Jones's Manor Farm. I had expressed my cautious respect for the fat, clever boar Napoleon, who excels in the art of persuasion. I paid special attention to the seven commandments that the animals had given themselves, written in white paint on a tarred wall – a kind of set of Tablets of the Law, binding on all living things. I dwelt on some of the laws, for instance the first of them: "Whatever goes upon two legs is an enemy." And the seventh as well: "All animals are equal."

I was pleased with my essay, and I waited impatiently for the exercise books to be given back. Stella didn't hesitate to give reasons for her marking in lessons when she returned our work, telling us why one essay was marked Satisfactory, another Poor, another Good – she had only once felt able to give an essay the mark Very Good. But she didn't arrive, several of her lessons were cancelled, and it wasn't easy to find out what was keeping her away from the school.

Heiner Thomsen knew where you lived; he wasn't in our class, but he came to Hirtshafen from Scharmünde every day. Stella had taken the room at the Seaview Hotel only for a few days in the holidays. I hoped to find her at home, and in spite of some misgivings I set out. I just had to know what was going on, or what had happened to her. Sometimes I wondered whether she was staying away from school because of me.

Next day I went to Scharmünde. I found the road where she lived, I found her house. The old man on the garden bench was sitting as if he had just knocked off work for the day, with a pipe in one hand and the handle of a walking stick in the other. When I opened the garden gate he raised his head – I saw a fleshy, badly shaved face – and looked at me with a smile. "Come closer," he said, "come closer, boy, or shouldn't I call you a boy?"

"That's all right," I said. "I'm still at school."

"Wouldn't think it to look at you," said the old radio operator, and after examining me critically for a moment he asked, "One of her students? My daughter's, I mean?"

"Frau Petersen is my English teacher," I said.

He was satisfied with that; I didn't have to say any more about the reason for my visit. He called, "Stella!" and again, turning his face to the open door, "Stella!"

She appeared. She didn't seem too surprised to find me with her father; perhaps she had seen me coming and was prepared for the moment when we would meet. Wearing jeans and a polo-necked shirt, she came out of the house and said, "I see you have a visitor, Dad." Her handshake gave no more away than a matter-of-fact greeting. "How nice to see you, Christian," she added formally. No displeasure, no reproof in her voice, and still less any surreptitious sign of delight.

Her father wanted to go indoors; it was getting too chilly for him and he needed her to support him. She pulled him to his feet, put an arm firmly round him and helped him away. Looking back over her shoulder, he told me, "Trouble with my backbone, a little souvenir of the past."

The old radio operator asked to be helped to his room, a small one with sunflowers nodding in at the window, which had a kind of workbench in front of it, and there was an old-fashioned sofa by the wall, with a rug carelessly thrown over it. The old man dropped heavily into a basket chair at the workbench and nodded to me, indicating that I should sit on a stool there.

"A ship in a bottle?" I asked, picking his handiwork up. A scene in harbour was immortalized inside the bottle, a big container ship in several colours being towed by a tug.

"My hobby," he said. "I pass the time that way. Sometimes I set myself problems, too." He pointed to a clear bottle with a sailing ship in it, its three masts lying flat on deck. "I'll have to get those up again," he said, adding that many people wondered how you got a three-master into a bottle. "But it's perfectly simple. First you fit the hull of the vessel in place, then you add the superstructure, the masts and rigging, and the artificial waves go in later as well."

As he talked about what he was doing, I listened to Stella's footsteps as she moved around the house, heard her telephoning, doing something in the kitchen, dealing with a visitor or delivery man at the front door. I was beginning to doubt whether I would get a chance of speaking to her alone at all when she came in with a tray and put it down on the workbench. I saw a large mug with the English words *The Gardener* on it, and a bottle of Captain Morgan's Rum. Her father took her hand, patted it, and said, "Thank you, my dear," adding to me, "Rum works wonders for a mug of tea." She did not leave him to help himself, but opened the bottle and poured a shot of rum into the tea. Then she patted her father's shoulder, said, "Your good health, Dad," in English, and then, firmly, to me, "There's something for you next door, Christian."

White-painted bookshelves, a green and white desk with several drawers, a leather-upholstered chaise longue, two wicker armchairs, and on the wall a large and puzzling reproduction of a picture: *A Queen Surveys Her Country.* On the desk, beside a stack of exercise books, stood a mug of tea, this one inscribed *The Friend.* I didn't particularly like your room, Stella, it seemed to me familiar, or at least I didn't feel as if I were entering strange territory. Alone with her, I embraced and kissed her, or rather I tried to kiss her, but she stiffened and resisted. "Not here, Christian, please, not here!" And when I put my hands under her polo shirt I also felt her resistance as she repeated, "Not here, Christian." I sat down, looked at the mug of tea, read aloud the words "The Friend", and indicated myself with a questioning gesture. Stella didn't answer. Instead, she asked, "Why did you come?"

At first I didn't know what to answer, but then I said, "I had to see you again, and anyway I wanted to suggest something."

With an expression of weary forbearance, Stella asked me to show consideration – consideration for her and other people as well. She asked me whether I'd thought how this relationship between us was going to work out: "Do you know what it means for me? And for you, too?"

"I couldn't stand it any more," I said. "I'd have waited outside the staffroom to see you again, even if it was just for a moment."

"Yes," she said, "but then what, Christian, or rather ask yourself calmly: now what?" You were letting me see that you had thought ahead, you had considered and anticipated what lay before us. "Now what?" is a question you ask in uncertainty, maybe in a mood of depression, or when you're completely at a loss. Suddenly she said, "Maybe I ought to get myself transferred to another school. It would make things a good deal easier for us."

"Then I'm coming with you."

"Oh, Christian." She shook her head, forbearance in her voice again, she seemed to feel nothing but regret at my remark. "Oh, Christian."

The stack of exercise books on her desk mesmerized me. I kept glancing surreptitiously at it. My essay was in there, she must have read it and marked it. When I thought of that I dared not touch Stella again, or ask what she thought of the essay.

As if reluctantly, her father suddenly called, "Stella!" and then again, like a request, "Stella!" She put the cigarette she had been about to light down on an ashtray and left me alone. Evidently the old radio operator was feeling chilly even at his workbench, he asked for his warm indoor jacket, then they whispered together and I knew it was about my visit. My exercise book with the essay wasn't on top of the pile, but even if it had been I wouldn't have picked it up. For behind the pile of exercise books on her desk stood a framed photograph of a blond, athletic man looking challengingly straight at the camera, threatening whoever was taking the picture with a rolled-up journal. On the margin of the photograph I read the words, in English: "Stella, with love. Colin."

Not right away, I didn't want to ask her right away who this Colin was and what linked her to him. I was trying to guess his age. He couldn't be so very much older than me. I picked up the cigarette lying on the ashtray and lit it, I looked at the picture of *A Queen Surveys Her Country*, it was by some English painter, I think his name was Attenborough. The queen's country was in twilight, no paths, no roads, you could just make out houses beside a stretch of water, low buildings out of reach.

Oh, your smile, Stella, when you came in and immediately saw that I was smoking your cigarette. With a movement of your hand, you told me to stay sitting where I was, this is different territory, you implied, it's not the classroom, you don't have to stand up here when I come in.

"He's feeling better," she said. "Today my father's feeling better."

She took a few steps, stopped in front of her desk and placed one hand on the pile of exercise books. I still dared not ask her opinion of my essay. She herself, I thought, must choose the moment. The longer her pause lasted, the more sure I was that I couldn't expect praise. She never withheld praise, she began with it every time she gave exercise books back, discussed our work and told us her reasons for our marks. I was waiting for her to sit down beside me, but she didn't, she went to the window and looked out. It was as if you were searching for something, Stella, something to say, an idea. After a while I saw the expression on her face changing, and with a touch of slight sorrow in her tone, not forbearance this time, she said, "What I'm doing now, Christian, is something I've never done before. You could call it subversive, yes, when I think of what links us, the school would see it as subversion. What I have to say to you ought to be only what is said in class." As she spoke I remembered that room in the Seaview Hotel, the pillow that we had shared, and I felt a vague fear and a vague pain, but only briefly, because after she had lit herself another cigarette she went back to pacing around the room.

What you said, Stella, didn't seem to be addressed to me personally at first. It was as if you wanted to express something as a matter of principle to anyone who might be concerned. "*Animal Farm* is a fable, an allegory, the story says one thing and also tells us another. Behind what we see going on in the foreground there's a wider truth; you could describe it as the story of the miseries of revolution." She stopped in front of the bookshelves and went on speaking as she looked at them. "The animals aren't so much thinking of the classic demands of revolutionaries – more bread, more freedom – their aim is to end the domination of human beings, a limited and concrete aim, and they achieve it. But then, with the founding of a new civilization, misery begins. It begins with the formation of social classes and certain individuals' aspirations to wield power."

Now Stella turned back to me. "And as we're on the subject, Christian, you gave an adequate account of the early chapters, the commandments, the slogans that you compared to the Tablets of the Law, all correct, perfectly accurate, and you quoted that terrible basic principle: 'All animals are equal, but some animals are more equal than others.' But you didn't mention the outcome of the revolution, or maybe you overlooked it, the outcome typical of so many revolutions. You didn't spot the power struggles in the ruling class, you missed the dreadful terror that set in after the conquest, and finally, Christian, you didn't notice that the whole thing is a portrayal of human behaviour. There's a book title – no reason why you should know it, but it says a great deal: *Revolution Eats Its Children*. In short, you named the causes of the revolution, but you hardly mentioned any of the reasons why it failed."

I didn't try to defend myself, I didn't do anything like that because I could see you knew more than I did, and everything you held against me was true. But there was one thing I thought I ought to know: what mark you had given me, or were going to give me. When I asked, "If I didn't write a good essay, I suppose I can't expect a very good mark," you shrugged your shoulders and said, in a tone with a touch of reproof in it, "I don't think this is the place to talk about marks."

Stella was letting me see that we ought to keep things separate, and that for all her affection for me, all her understanding of what we had done, she wasn't ready to give up authority in her own field. We ought not to talk about marks, she had said, so firmly that I made no attempt to persuade her to change her mind, and nor did I venture to put my hands on her hips and pull her down on my lap.

When the telephone rang you didn't want me to leave your study, you looked at me as you spoke, you were amused, relieved, this was the call you had been waiting for. It seemed that Stella's friends, who had been going to take her on board their yacht ages ago, were ringing again to say they were on their way. As far as I could make out, they didn't yet know what day they would arrive; the wind was against them. But when I suggested going out to show her the underwater stone-fields again, she said no. "Later," she said. "When I come back." And when we parted she said this had been a very surprising visit, certainly intending to indicate that she would rather do without such surprises in future. In her front garden, I turned to look back, and they were both waving to me, Stella and the old radio operator.

Alone now, alone in my classroom, I sat in front of the open drawer and looked at Stella's picture. I decided to tell her everything she didn't yet know about me, including the accident by the breakwater that nearly happened when I was checking the way the stones lay and saw a huge boulder coming down right above me; it would have hit me but for the pressure wave that flung me out of its way.

The door opened, so quietly that I didn't hear it. "There you are," said Heiner Thomsen, quickly coming over to me. He had a message from Herr Block; the principal wanted to speak to me at once.

"Do you know what he wants?"

"No idea."

"Where is he?"

"Same place as usual."

I closed the drawer, and slowly went downstairs to Block's room on the ground floor. He did not come forward to meet me; sitting at his desk, he signed to me to come closer. The way he was looking at me – that penetrating, questioning look – told me at once that he expected something special of me. I felt it was humiliating for me to be left standing there so long in silence. His narrow lips moved, he seemed to be tasting something; finally he said, "You obviously wanted to conclude our hour of remembrance in your own way."

"Me?"

"You took Frau Petersen's photograph away."

"Who says so?"

"A number of people saw you. They were watching when you picked up the photograph, put it under your pullover and took it away."

"They must be wrong."

"No, Christian, they are not wrong, and now please will you tell me why you did it? Frau Petersen was your English teacher."

I was prepared to admit that I'd taken Stella's picture, but standing there in front of his desk I couldn't think of any reason to offer him, least of all the only reason why I did it. After a moment I said, "All right, I'll admit I took the photograph. I didn't want it to get lost, maybe, I wanted to keep it as a memento of my teacher. We all liked her in my class."

"But, Christian, you wanted to keep the photograph to yourself, didn't you?"

"It ought to be in our classroom," I said.

He listened to that with an ironic smile, and then repeated, "In your classroom. I see. Why not in the school hall, on the board with pictures of several former members of our staff? Why not there?"

"I can put it there if you like," I said. "I'll do that right away."

Now Block was looking at me very gravely, and I was inclined to think he knew more than I'd assumed, although I couldn't imagine how far his knowledge went, or what exactly he suspected me of. Nothing annoys me so much as being suspected of something and not knowing what. To put a stop to this conversation, I suggested doing what he wanted here and now. "If it's all right, then, Dr Block, I'll go and put the photograph where you want it to be."

He nodded. I was dismissed. I was already at the door when he called me back again. He did not meet my eyes as he said, "What we do not say, Christian, sometimes has more consequences than what we do say. Do you understand what I mean?"

"Yes, I understand," I said, and I made haste to get Stella's photo up where he wanted it.

Once again, Stella, I carried your photo under my pullover. On my way to the hall I didn't speak to anyone I passed, indeed I avoided them. The board wasn't quite full; six photos of former teachers were up there, all of them old men; there was only one who looked as if he might have a sense of humour, a teacher in naval uniform with two crossed signalling flags in front of his chest. He was said to have taught biology, long before my time. I put Stella's photo up between him and a man with a craggy face. I didn't stop to bother about assessing the company she'd be keeping. You had your place, Stella, and that was enough for me just then.

Looking at you brought back to me something that I needed, or thought I needed: the sudden happiness of a touch, the joy that demanded a repeat performance. I was sure, in that moment, that I had needed that photograph of you all for myself. The brightness on the beach, the dazzling brightness that Sunday when I was waiting for Stella in the Volkswagen Beetle that Claus Bultjohan had lent me. It was a cabriolet and belonged to his father, who was away in Scandinavia on a TV assignment, making a film about the culture of the Lapps who, as nomads, astonishingly had the right to cross the Russian border. After my visit to her home, I hadn't even tried to make a date to meet Stella. Knowing that in this spell of settled summer weather she would come to the beach on her own to read or sunbathe, I decided to wait for her at a suitable distance from her house. I listened to Benny Goodman in the car. I drove very slowly after her as she walked along, wearing her brightly coloured blue and yellow beach dress, with her beach bag hanging from a strap over her shoulder. She walked fast and confidently; I stopped suddenly beside her just before she reached the kiosk where she bought smoked fish and magazines. I saw the displeasure in her face, but that expression immediately gave way to surprise and amazement. "Oh, Christian," was all she said. I opened the car door, and after a moment's hesitation she got in.

She promptly sat down on my camera, which I had put on the passenger seat, "Good heavens, what's that?"

"Won it in a competition," I said. "I came fifth."

"Where are you taking it?" she asked, to which I replied, "Anywhere there's something worth seeing."

We stopped down at the place where the navigation marks had been brought in for their new coat of paint, though they still had to be freed from rust first. How cheerfully you agreed to my idea of taking some photographs here, sitting on the navigation marks, riding on them, clutching them, you played along in almost exuberant spirits, and seemed to be caressing a lifebuoy. Only when I asked you be a radiator mascot did you dismiss the idea. I thought of you sitting on the radiator, just like those pretty girls in car showrooms, when the breeze lifted your beach-dress, and your pale blue panties showed. You quickly waved to me to stop, and said, "Not that, Christian, let's not go as far as that," and then you asked where I was going to have the film developed. I promised her to keep the photos to myself and not show them to anyone else.

Stella photographed me just once that Sunday. We were sitting in the fish restaurant beside the casino; almost all the places on the terrace in the sun were taken. Stella read the menu several times, and her way of coming to a decision amused me; no sooner had she closed the leather-bound menu than she reached for it again, read it, shook her head and changed her mind. It didn't escape her that her search of the menu, her decision and then her change of mind amused me, because before she ordered she said, "I sometimes like not being sure, I like to be able to choose." We ordered plaice wrapped in bacon and fried, with potato salad on the side.

She admired my skill in cutting up the fish, particularly the long incision with which I separated the back fillet from the underside, and tried to copy me, but she failed, and I pulled her plate towards me and did it for her. Stella watched, interested, as I then picked up the skeleton of the fish, licked it carefully clean, with relish, and held it up in front of my face. Stella laughed out loud, turned away, looked back at me, smiling, and said, "Wonderful, Christian, stay just like that, we have to put this on record." She took a photo of me, wanting me to open my mouth and put the bones against my lips, and then she took the shot again. When I suggested that we could take a picture of both of us together she hesitated for a moment, as I had expected. Finally she agreed, and after lunch we went down to the beach and found a place among abandoned sand castles. Then we took a photo of ourselves with the delayed-action shutter release. Neither Stella nor I thought that what the photograph showed, or rather would show, was anything to worry about. We were sitting on the beach in summer clothes, close together, we were taking care to look happy, or at least pleased with ourselves. I didn't say so, but I was thinking: I love Stella. And I was also thinking: I'd like to know more about her. You can never know enough when you realize you love someone. While you took Faulkner's *Light in August* out of your beach bag, stretched out, and told me, as if by way of apology, that you really had to read this writer, I asked you, "Why? Why do you have to read him? He's not going to be one of our set books, is he?"

"He's my favourite author," you said. "Well, one of my favourite authors this summer."

"What do you see in him that's so special?"

"Do you really want to know?"

"I want to know everything about you," I said, and without stopping to think much about it you initiated me into the world of Faulkner, his celebration of the Mississippi wilderness where bear and stag reigned supreme, the opossum and the moccasin snake were at home, before the land was transformed by the saw and the coming of cotton mills. But you also told me about his characters: the masters and the scoundrels who imposed their own law on the wilderness, contributing to the fate of the South.

I liked listening to her; she didn't speak as she did in class, she was more hesitant, not playing the teacher now, her way of talking flattered me. I could almost have been her colleague. Naturally I made up my mind to read her favourite author at the first chance I got, or at least try to read him. We lay there side by side in silence for some time; I turned towards her and looked at her face. Her eyes were closed. Stella's face looked to me even more beautiful than it had on the pillow, and now and then I detected the hint of a smile. Although I'd have liked to know what she was thinking about, I asked no questions; just once, I did ask her who that man Colin was, and she said briefly a fellow-student from her teacher training college who was now teaching at a school in Bremen. But once I thought I did know what she was thinking of, when an expectant expression appeared on her face. I suspected she was thinking of me, and she confirmed that idea of mine by placing a hand on my stomach. You can think of someone even if he's there beside you.

Who spotted us I'm not sure. Maybe it was Heiner Thomsen or one of his gang coming down to the beach to play volleyball. Their voices announced their arrival. But suddenly the voices died away, and next moment I saw several figures looking for cover behind the sand castles, ducking low as they crept up to us. They wanted to see anything there was to see, anything they could talk about at school. I didn't need to point out my classmates to Stella; she had noticed them already, and she just winked at me, stood up, and strolled towards the sand castles. One of them stood up straight, then two more of them, and three, they stood there looking awkward, as if caught in the act of doing something wrong. One of them managed to say hello. Stella inspected them cheerfully, and said, as if she didn't take offence at the way they had crept up in secret, "Sometimes it's nice to spend an hour on the beach. Anyone who wants to join in is welcome." No one did want to join in.

I admired you so much at that moment, Stella, and I could have hugged you when you accepted their invitation to play volleyball with them. They clapped, delighted, and both teams wanted to have you on their side. Only you, all I could do was watch you, and I instinctively thought about sharing a pillow with you again, or feeling your breasts on my back as we embraced. Although you were the mainstay of your team – no one served as well as you did, no one smashed the ball so precisely – you were defeated.

They tried to persuade Stella to play in the next round too, but she declined in a friendly way, saying she had to go home.

My classmates stood around the car, watching as Stella put her seat belt on and giving me ironic advice, and one of two of them whistled after us as we drove off. We went straight to her house. The old radio operator wasn't sitting on the garden seat; two windows were open. I switched off the engine, expecting her to ask me in. As she said nothing, I suggested taking our inflatable out to the stone-fields. Stella drew me to her and kissed me. She said, "My friends have arrived; they're going to pick me up and take me on board."

"When?"

"It could be tomorrow. I hope so, anyway. I need a few days to myself."

"Later, then?"

"Yes, Christian, later."

Before she got out of the car, she kissed me again, and waved to me from the front door, not fleetingly, not casually, but slowly and as if she were telling me to resign myself to our parting. Maybe she wanted to console me too. That was when I first thought of living with Stella. It was a sudden bold idea, and today I know that in many ways it was inappropriate, an idea born only from the fear that my link with Stella might come to an end. How naturally such a longing for something to last arises.

Hirtshafen seemed to me a dreary place from the day they took you on board their two-master. Sonja had been watching, and I discovered from her that they sent a dinghy out to the beach to pick you up and take you over to the *Pole Star*. Apparently the owner hadn't been able to think of a more original name for his yacht. You had gone. I wandered around and sat on the rusting navigation marks for some time, I sat by the three pines and on the wooden bridge, and I went into the Seaview Hotel without knowing what I would do there. One afternoon I thought of going to see Stella's father, but I couldn't think of a reason for any such visit. I just wanted to visit him because I hoped to feel near Stella. Then her letter came.

I had been cleaning our *Katarina*. I'd come home tired from working on her, when my father said, "There's a letter for you, Christian. From Denmark." I went straight up to my room; I wanted to be alone with it. The sender's address was written with a flourish and as if to conceal something; it ran only: Stella P., Ärö Island. I realized at once that, given this vague phrasing, no answer was expected. I didn't read her letter from the start; first I had to know how she signed it, and I was happy when I read, in English: "Hope to see you soon, best wishes, Stella." I was so happy that the first thing I did was to think where I would keep her letter.

You wrote about calm seas, about a good time bathing in a quiet bay, and your party's visit to a Museum of Oceanography on another island. There had been so much to see: the skeleton of a ray, the skeleton of a whale – a huge blue whale that had been stranded on the shore – and several aquariums full of parrot-fish and corals and little rose-fish. You had particularly liked – and I couldn't help grinning when I read this bit – a couple of king crabs eating a filleted herring. You called them the most lethargic feeders in all creation; it was a real test of patience to watch them having their dinner. You mentioned the sea-horses as well, and how they looked to you like contented little creatures. In the end I couldn't think of anywhere better to hide Stella's letter than in my English grammar, and as I folded it up and put it inside the textbook I thought ahead, without knowing what would happen I thought of some indefinite day, and imagined ourselves looking back and asking, "Do you remember?" Then, sitting side by side, we would read her letter together, perhaps surprised to find how much cause for merriment it gave us.

It was at this time that I first dreamed of Stella, a dream that made me think. In the dream I arrived late at school, the others were already sitting there, and turned to me grinning, smirking and expectant; when I was sitting down they made me look at the board. The words on the board said in block letters, in English: Please come back, dear Stella, Christian is waiting for you. I rushed to the board and wiped the words away. The sly pleasure on their faces told me that they thought they had won a skirmish.

Waiting, waiting for your return; although I sometimes thought I was doomed to waiting, and I was used to it by now, it seemed to me particularly difficult in Stella's absence. I took guests at the Seaview Hotel out in the afternoons in our *Katarina*, almost always to Bird Island, where a small landing stage had been built. I guided my passengers around the island, showed them the bird warden's hut, told them about the old man who liked his solitary life, and sometimes shared it with a tame seagull that had once been injured by a shot and couldn't fly any more.

Even as the man got in and paid for the trip, he seemed familiar to me, and later – he found himself a seat in the stern – I was almost sure of it: he was that Colin whose photo I'd seen in Stella's room.

He was wearing a linen jacket over a check shirt, he bore a remarkable similarity to Colin, and only when he spoke, turning to the stout lady sitting next to him and explaining something to her with a wealth of gestures – probably what to do when a ship capsizes – did I begin to doubt it, although only fleetingly, because as soon as he looked keenly at me in a rather self-conscious way I was sure he was Colin, and he had turned up here in the hope of seeing Stella. "Stella with love, Colin." He helped the older passengers to get out on the landing stage, and during our tour of the island he asked more questions than anyone else. He told us he collected gulls' eggs, and would have liked to find a few here, but it wasn't the season.

It was not in the hut but on the tree trunk that had been washed up, where we were sitting watching the waves coming in on the beach, that he began to suffer from breathlessness; first he cleared his throat, then he put his head back and gasped for air, clutching his throat, and fighting for breath with violent swallowing movements. He was looking at me now not keenly, but in need of help, and he searched his pockets, patting them to find something.

"Aren't you well?" I asked.

"My spray," he said, adding, "Sanastmax, I left my spray in the hotel."

I asked the passengers, but not many of them

wanted to go back to the hotel yet, so I got him on board and took him back to the Seaview Hotel. The receptionist led the man, who was still breathing heavily, to a sofa and asked what he needed – "It's on the bedside table, my inhaler is on the bedside table" – took a key from the board where they hung with a practised gesture, and quickly climbed the stairs. Alone with the man who looked like Colin, and whom I had momentarily taken for Colin, I decided to find out for certain; I drew up a chair and sat down beside him, dismissing the thanks he was expressing, with difficulty. I told him about our party, the Hirtshafen beach party, saying he could have joined in if he'd only been here a little earlier, people had come from all over the place, I said, even my teachers didn't want to miss the Hirtshafen beach party. It didn't interest him, he didn't want to know any more about it, but I still had a feeling that he sometimes cast me an inquiring glance. However, the man at reception settled the matter. When he came back with the inhaler he said, "There was a phone call for you, Dr Cranz, a call from Hanover. The car is coming tomorrow." Although something in me had surprised him early that morning, his mind wasn't on me; apparently he didn't remember any meeting.

Back at home I re-read Stella's letter, I read it several times, and thinking of the bird warden's hut I decided to write to Stella, I simply had to. Without any hesitation I wrote, "Dearest Stella," and told her at once how dreary everything here in Hirtshafen was without her, "too many old people, boring boat trips that smell of fish all the time, and the wind never changes, it's always a cool easterly." And then I told her about my idea. As I wrote I felt more and more enthusiastic, even happy about it. I outlined my plan for the two of us. "Imagine, Stella: we could move into the bird warden's hut, just you and me, I'll put up a notice on the landing stage saying No Landing Here. I'll repair the roof and put a bolt on the door, collect firewood for the stove, I'll buy some cans of food and dried stuff from our marine stores. We won't go short of anything," I wrote. Finally there was the prospect of swimming together, and best of all, from the moment we woke up we'd be there for each other. I thought of a P.S., and added: "Maybe we could learn how to live together." At first I was going to sign it in English with "Yours sincerely", but then I decided on "Yours truly, Christian." I put the letter in an envelope and slipped it into the English grammar textbook, for later.

While I was still thinking about the letter, my father called me downstairs, a brief call in a voice used to giving orders. He was standing at the open window with his field-glasses in his hand, and he pointed out into the bay. "Take a look at that, Christian." Our barge was drifting there, and not far from it our tug *Endurance*. The two vessels were connected by a line that was not taut but hung loose, dipping into the water. Looking through the field-glasses, I could see that our barge was carrying a heavy load of rocks. I could also make out Frederik on the tug, standing at the stern and manipulating a boathook, pushing and shoving.

"Come on," said my father, and we went down to the landing stage where our inflatable was lying. I took us out, and we tied up to the tug.

My father was soon in the picture. Frederik hardly needed to tell him that the tug had run into a fish-trap unmarked by flags, and become entangled, before he was handing me the diving mask and onboard knife. "You go down and take a look." The tug's propeller, turning furiously, had worked its way into the trap, pulled it over itself, and was now crippled, strangulated and with part of the trap hanging loose from it. Without surfacing to tell them what the scene looked like underwater, I set to work with the knife right away. There was a mackerel caught in the net; it had shot in like a torpedo and choked to death. I cut it out and went on carving away at the hard, apparently waxed cord of which the trap consisted, coming up for air now and then. If our onboard knife had had a serrated edge, I could have freed the propeller from the tangled trap more easily, but as things were I had to push and press the knife hard until I finally managed to cut the tangles away. My father and Frederik praised my work, consulted briefly and agreed on what to do next.

The engine of our tug was reliable. Slowly, very slowly, we got under way. The slack line to the barge rose from the water, stretched taut, and there was enough traction on it for the barge to move, turn, and follow the course of the tug. I thought we'd be taking this last load to the mouth of the harbour, to add to the rocks shoring up the breakwater, but my father had decided against that. We threw out the anchor before reaching the breakwater, Frederik went to the winch, and as usual raised rock after rock into the air, swung them overboard and let them sink. He didn't send me down to check the way the stones were lying; it was enough for my father to deposit them on the bottom there so that, as he said, they would break the first onslaught of the waves coming in, thus checking their full impact on the breakwater at the harbour mouth. Our work didn't immediately seem to be having much effect, but when we'd sunk almost the whole cargo of rocks, the movement of the waves coming in at a leisurely pace changed; they rose and broke, tumbling into one another, levelled out, rippling, and lost so much strength that they dispersed as if exhausted, without the strength to gather their forces and rise high again.

A rowing boat came into view near Bird Island, moving with slow oar-strokes and apparently making for Hirtshafen, but only for a while; it unexpectedly turned in our direction, and the oarsman waved a couple of times, indicating that he wanted to tie up to us. My father lowered his field-glasses. "It's Mathiessen, the old bird warden," he said, and signed to me to help the man on board. Falling easily into conversation, he and my father spoke each other's first names and shook hands. Wilhelm? Andreas? was their sole form of greeting. They were old friends. Over a rum, they asked one another about their families, their future plans and their health, and that was when I learned that Mathiessen had finally retired. "I'm packing it in, Wilhelm, it's my arthritis. The place will be unmanned for now." He had just been to his hut for the last time, he said, to fetch a few personal items and his reports on the last year there: "There wasn't much happened." They talked about a naval rescue exercise out at sea in which a soldier had died, and then my father told me to tow Mathiessen back to Hirtshafen. He sat in the inflatable beside me, his pipe in his crooked, arthritic fingers as if he were defending it from attack, and closed his eyes now and then. He didn't seem surprised when I asked him what was going to happen to his hut now, just shrugged his shoulders. Was he planning to sell it, I asked, to which he replied, "Such things aren't for sale, Christian."

"Is it going to stay there, then?"

"Might as well, so far as I'm concerned. It could come in useful, a place for someone to go, take shelter there."

"Shelter?"

"From bad weather, yes."

"People don't so easily lose their way and end up there."

"Don't be so sure, there's been folk in the hut not long ago. Could be they wanted shelter, could be they just wanted time alone together. I notice that sort of thing right away, I can feel it." He nodded, as if to confirm what he said.

"And does anything ever go missing?" I asked.

"Never," he said, "I've never yet known anything go missing, and that makes me think. Sometimes people leave something behind, a handkerchief, a half-eaten chocolate bar, a slide for a woman's hair, but those who want to be alone there have never taken anything, boy, that's the way it is."

He had cast out a trolling line as we crossed the water, a long line with two wobblers on it. At the harbour entrance he pulled it in and was pleased to have caught two garfish. After I had made fast his boat he gave me the two fish, saying, "Take them home, Christian, I expect your mother will pickle them in aspic, garfish in aspic, that's the thing to do with them. See you, then," he added, clapping me on the shoulder by way of goodbye.

The photo of Stella and me among the sandcastles on the beach had been in my room for several days, and my mother didn't seem to have noticed it, or at least she didn't examine it for any length of time or ask questions. However, she did once turn it towards the light, and looked at it inquiringly – that was the day when I was making my way through one of Orwell's essays. She was about to put it down again when something about it suddenly struck her. She sat down by my window, brought the photograph close to her eyes, looked at me and then back at the photo. The way her gaze switched from it to me and back again, I could tell she was trying to find something out that she didn't yet know. A clouded expression appeared on her face; she was obviously registering the fact that she no longer knew everything about me – as she always used to – and in a certain sense she had lost me. She always wanted to know everything, no doubt because when I was a little boy she had wanted to spare me disappointments and pain and mistakes. She spent ages looking at the photo in silence; I couldn't think that it gave away anything much, and was about to say something, when she finally commented, in her usual thoughtful way, "She looks older than you, Christian. The woman in the photo beside you. I mean."

"She's my English teacher," I said. "We met by chance on the beach."

"Pretty woman," said my mother, adding, "Does she have any children?"

"As far as I know she's not married."

"A very pretty woman," my mother repeated.

After that observation, I ventured to suggest, "If you don't mind, I'll bring her home for coffee some day."

"Your teacher?" asked my mother, surprised.

"Why not?" I said. "I'm sure she'll come if I invite her, she's very nice."

"I can see she is," said my mother, adding, "And you like each other. I can see that too." Without another word, she put the photo back in its place, caressed my hair, and left me alone.

How she knew more than she was letting on was her own secret. Or if she didn't know, she guessed, she sensed it. They were talking about me in bed, and I could hear them through the door, which happened to be not quite shut. They had come home late.

My father hadn't noticed the photo yet, and at first it didn't seem to surprise him that I had a picture of Stella and myself standing on my desk. "Oh, come on, Jutta," he said, "these things happen all the time. Every boy wants to admire someone, and it's all the more likely if this teacher is pretty."

"If only it were just admiration," said my mother. "I've nothing against admiration, but it's more than that with Christian, believe me, it's more than that."

"What makes you think so?"

"The way they're sitting happily on the beach, hand in hand, he's hand in hand with his teacher, and the way they're looking at each other. You'd think they'd just been waiting for one another."

"Maybe Christian took a bit of a fancy to her, that'll be all. I know his teacher; she's very good-looking."

"In that picture you'd think they were about to fall into each other's arms any moment. I really do think you should take this seriously."

"Christian is eighteen, Jutta."

"Yes, well," said my mother, "and this teacher is considerably older."

"So? A difference in age is sometimes an advantage."

I couldn't help smiling to myself when, after a pause, he said in a different and amused voice, "We both discussed that once ourselves, a long time ago."

Even after this reference to some shared

experience of theirs, my mother's mind didn't seem to have been set at rest. She mentioned Christine, my friend at school, who had called several times to invite me to a barbecue and always went away disappointed. My father took his time before replying. "Sometimes you just don't know what hit you, you're defenceless." I instinctively sat up in bed – I'd never heard my father talk like that before – and I was thinking of opening the door a little wider, but I didn't, because it seemed that was all they had to say, and they wished each other good night.

It won't surprise you, Stella, that I picked up our photo first thing next morning to look for signs of what my mother thought she had seen in it, but I couldn't see anything to confirm her suspicions.

As if it would bring me closer to Stella, I went back to Orwell's essays. I admit that I didn't know the background well enough to understand everything he was saying, but what he wrote about the critics' reception of *Animal Farm* made me think. He had expected his book to be understood as a parable about the rise and theory and practice of all dictatorships – with one exception: the Russian dictatorship, which mustn't be exposed to comparisons showing it in a bad light. I decided to talk to Stella not just about that but also – like Orwell himself – about the freedom of the press in extreme situations, for instance during a war. I imagined all of us discussing the subject in class, and all the students being invited to give their opinions. It never happened.

And I remembered the time recently when sleepy little Hirtshafen woke up; all of a sudden it rose to the rank of a conference centre. Fisheries experts from seven nations met here to discuss the projects closest to their hearts, come to an agreement on them, and most important of all to work out models to present to their governments. The experts – two of them of ministerial rank – stayed at the Seaview Hotel, and a green VW transporter van decked out with flags stood outside the hotel day and night.

I could never have dreamed that, during this event, Stella would acknowledge me publicly for once, not with words but with a gesture. She had been asked to act as interpreter for the Scottish expert, standing in for his simultaneous translator, who had gone down with flu. Pleased, but a little apprehensive, she told me about this assignment. She was apprehensive because, she said, she had to confess she didn't know enough about fish species. "You see, Christian, there's always a chance to learn something new." And she made sure she knew the English names of gurnard, flounder and pike-perch. Herring and mackerel in English were very much the same as their German counterparts and presented no problems. The reception to mark the opening of the conference surprised me for more than one reason: the fisheries experts from seven nations greeted one another at length, as exuberantly as if they had really missed each other badly and the joy of their reunion called for particularly strong expression. All that hand-shaking, clapping one another on the back, hugs and exclamations: you'd have thought it was a long-anticipated family party in progress on the terrace of the Seaview Hotel.

When the delegation began moving into the large conference room – Stella had asked me to be there as well, saying "Just come along and listen," – I followed a couple walking arm in arm. Both had badges with Norwegian names pinned to their lapels, showing a leaping fish, probably a sea trout. Stella too was wearing a badge with her name on it. Before I entered the conference room I felt a firm grip on my upper arm. I was taken aside, and a tall security man asked me, in a not unfriendly tone, "Are you a delegate?" As I did not reply at once, he signed to a colleague to join him. The second security man took my wrist and, with the words, "Don't give us any trouble now!" was about to lead me away to a corner full of house-plants. Stella had seen this episode, and came purposefully towards us. In a tone of voice I had never heard from her before, she tapped her own name badge and told the two men sharply, "This is my adviser, so kindly let go of him at once." You took my hand, and the two representatives of law and order looked at each other undecidedly, but they did let go of me, and we walked into the big room as if we belonged together. I found a chair in the front row with a good view of the platform, and Stella went up on it to join her delegate, a Scottish fisheries expert who sported side-whiskers and looked relaxed.

A Norwegian expert opened the conference by welcoming the company in almost melodious English, as "My dear friends and colleagues." Through his interpreter, he announced the good news that the latest ruling on quotas for herring fishing in the North Sea had had the expected result. This information was received with applause; I got the impression that all present had contributed to the successful outcome. Two more short papers followed, one given by the Scottish expert who, speaking with the help of key points that he had noted down, mentioned the precarious state of eel fishing today; he felt obliged, he said, to predict that the eel would soon disappear from our waters if we did not introduce measures to protect it. He blamed this situation not only on unauthorized fishing for eel but also on the changing Atlantic currents that no longer brought us the little elvers from the Sargasso Sea. Stella had to ask what he meant only once or twice; she sometimes got around a problem by paraphrasing his English, as I noticed from her hesitation and then the extra number of words she used. The Scottish expert thanked her by making her a little bow and giving her a piece of paper. I assumed it was a written note of congratulation, but later I discovered that the Scotsman was good at doing lightning sketches, and as he spoke had been drawing Stella as a mermaid with a prettily curving fish-tail. You looked like some fairy-tale beauty, Stella, and I would have followed you anywhere, even to the bottom of the sea.

Later, it was the Scottish expert again who announced a break by pointing to the buffet, its dishes until now covered by cloths, and saying in English, "The bazaar is open!"

Stella nodded to him, and we went over to the buffet together. She ignored my compliment. As if it were her job, she took my plate, enumerated the dishes on offer, and filled it with little tasters. What a choice! There were at least twelve different kinds of herring dishes alone: in aspic, with herbs, smoked, baked, and of course *matjes*, soused herring. There were also herring fillets rolled up with pieces of gherkin, and herring fillets with slices of hard-boiled egg. In addition, there were glistening pink pieces of salmon, fillets of halibut, and dark red diced tuna. Fillets of sole were also on offer, along with rolled fillets of hake and pale pieces of monkfish. In fact, all the bounty of the sea was served up to the fisheries experts of those seven countries, and the absence of eel did not surprise me. Once I bumped into the Scottish expert, who glanced appreciatively at my plate and, having made a civil apology, asked if I was "a native fisherman"; when I said, also in English, "We only fish for stones," he laughed, obviously thinking it was a joke.

It did not escape me that he was seeking Stella's company. Whoever he was talking to, he kept looking past that person or over his head in search of Stella. Over the steamed mackerel that we were eating at a tall table, she showed me his lightning sketch; he had drawn her with long hair and large, dreamy eyes, and at the sight of your curving fishtail covered with scales, Stella, I had to touch you there and then. She did not withdraw her hand from mine, but waved casually to a Polish fisheries expert – "Just coming, with you in a moment" – and as she turned away she said to me, "This evening, Christian, I'll be expecting you, just tap on the window." And looking down at the witty portrait of herself, she added, smiling, "Come and see me this evening."

The fisheries experts enjoyed a musical interlude, welcoming a singer who had been engaged by their chairman. Accompanying himself on his guitar, he sang about their own element, the oceans which were the subject of their longing and their concern, conjuring up the sea and the wind and, not least, an anxious mother waiting for the return home of her nearest and dearest from far away. They applauded in time to the music. Stella clapped as well, but when several of the fisheries experts later went to the bar, she did not go with them.

After a short conversation with one of the delegates, who thought he had met me at the Fisheries Biological Institute in Bergen, I noticed that Stella was not in the big room any longer. I left the Seaview Hotel, walked along the beach and then down the coastal path at my leisure; I wanted to give her time. Full of anticipation, I decided to talk to Stella about the future, our future, I would tell her my own plans for a life together. I had made those plans without really stopping to think, for I thought I had a right to believe that my feelings would last. So I set off on the way to Scharmünde. There was a light on in Stella's room, a little reading lamp, but she herself wasn't there. I climbed over the low garden fence, slipped in among the sunflowers and looked in at the kitchen. I saw them both there. Stella was pouring something liquid from a casserole into a small dish, and the old radio operator sat on a bench watching her expectantly. As she worked, she said something briefly to him now and then, as if to calm his impatience. I was surprised by the attentive way her father watched her, particularly when she began cutting bread. It looked like a heavy, farm-style loaf, and she cut off the crusts, pressing her lips together in concentration. She stood above the loaf, setting the knife at a well-judged angle and pressing, pressing hard, sometimes sticking her lower lip out and blowing air up into her face. She placed the bread and the dish in front of her father, sat down with him, and watched him eating. He ate quickly, with what looked like the good appetite or even the greed of old age. Perhaps to commend him, she patted him gently on the shoulder, and when he crumbled his last slice of bread over the dish, she kissed his forehead. The old radio operator reached for her hand, and held it in his for a moment without a word.

I left my place among the sunflowers, walked round the house, cast one more glance into Stella's room, and then set off along the path home, in what was now the twilight, at peace with myself and with my intention of writing to her at once to say why I hadn't tapped at her window after all. I couldn't; with the picture of that scene in the kitchen before my eyes, I couldn't do it.

I was still writing when someone scratched at

my door – didn't knock but scratched, the way dogs or cats do when they want to be let in.

Sonja was standing outside the door, barefoot and wearing her sleeveless dress. My little neighbour didn't say hello, she just walked in, as she so often did, and when I said, "You ought to have been in bed long ago,", she replied, "I'm on my own at home." She came over to my desk, very self-assured, got up on the chair, smiled, and put something down. "It's for you, Christian. I found it for you." A piece of amber lay there in front of the photo of Stella and me, its edges clouded, but clear and shining at the centre.

"Did you find it on the beach?"

"It was hanging in a seaweed plant – the seaweed had come loose."

I gave Sonja my magnifying glass, and she looked at the amber, examining it very closely through the glass. Of cause she knew what can be found in amber, and as if she had expected or hoped for it, she cried, "Oh yes, Christian, there's something inside it."

The magnifying glass passed back and forth between us. Our search was successful, as we agreed. "A beetle, Christian, a little beetle!"

"A fly as well," I added. "They weren't either of them watching out when the hurricane broke, and now they're caught in the amber for ever."

That was enough for her. She was satisfied with my explanation, and was less interested in the captive insects than in the photograph of Stella and me. Picking it up, she said, "That's your teacher, right?"

"Yes, Sonja, that's my teacher Frau Petersen."

She spent a long time working out what the photo told her, and suddenly asked, "Do you love each other?"

"Why do you ask?"

"Well, if you love each other, Christian, they're sure to make you repeat a year at school."

"Oh, I think I'll manage to move up, all the same," I said.

"I'll soon have her as my teacher too."

"That's something to look forward to, Sonja. Lessons with her are fun."

"Suppose she comes to live here, can I still come to see you?"

"Always. You can always come to see us."

She thought about that, and my relationship with Stella seemed to occupy her mind so much that I was sure there was more she wanted to ask, but then someone called her. I recognized her mother's voice at once, a shrill, unattractive voice which, I sometimes thought, upset even the waterfowl in the bay. I thanked Sonja for the amber, and promised to keep it next to the photograph.

Alone again, I took my savings book out of the drawer. It was a long time since I'd touched the savings book, which had been a confirmation present. It came with the sum of a hundred marks, and now contained two hundred and forty. I decided to draw out a hundred and fifty marks. I didn't yet know what I would need the money for, I just wanted to have it with me in case I needed it.

My father suspected that I had secret requirements of my own when we were on the barge, and I suggested he might pay me more regularly and more generously for my work in the holidays and after school. On our way home together – we were sitting on deck smoking – I asked if we could work out fixed prices for my work: the expeditions with the *Katarina* and my work on the barge. He'd never before looked at me with such surprise: surprise and suspicion too. At first he asked, "What do you need the money for?" And as I didn't answer that question, he asked how I thought he ought to pay me. I told him I'd be happy with five marks for an expedition in the *Katarina*, and I thought another five for doing a job on the barge would be suitable. He looked as if he were calculating the sums I'd mentioned; perhaps comparing them with the wages he paid Frederik – and I knew what those came to – but anyway, he didn't object, and after a while he asked, "But I suppose you intend to go on living with us, Christian, don't you?" The touch of irony in his voice didn't escape me, and I couldn't think what to say in answer; I was relieved that he didn't press the point. He looked at me encouragingly, nudged me in the ribs, said, "Come on," and we landed and walked home the usual way. When we were passing the boathouse he put a hand on my shoulder and left it there until we reached our front door. Then he seemed to remember that there was something on his mind, something he still had to settle, and we went back to the boathouse. He led me in, and in silence we went over to the ladder that led up to a small loft.

At that moment I knew what it was: he had discovered my hiding place behind the ropes and nets and bamboo poles, and he wanted me to explain the stuff I was hoarding there. It amounted to a few cans of food, two bags of flour, dried fruit, noodles and some ship's biscuit. Anyone looking at it was bound to assume I planned to go on quite a long voyage. My father pointed to the stock of provisions I had secretly assembled, and said, with pretended admiration, "Well, that should keep you going in your own household for a while, I guess."

This time I did think of an answer. I told him there was to be a big class outing, and we were going to stay in tents on a campsite for a few days. He smiled, and I wasn't sure whether he believed me or not. When we weren't so close, and he was on his way down the ladder, he came back to my financial suggestion in a casual tone of voice. "That's all right, Christian, just keep a record of the hours you work."

~

Frederik always had a hip flask with him; whether he was working on the barge or the tug, whether he was sitting on the bench outside the boat-house or going out to Bird Island, from time to time he would put his hand in his pocket, bring out the hip flask and raise it to his lips. The flask was made of metal in a leather case, and was filled with his favourite rum. He certainly had it with him the afternoon when he overturned the inflatable abeam of the Seaview Hotel in a rising wind, and gave the spectators watching from the wooden bridge an entertaining story to tell about their holidays. I had no doubt that the inflatable had been lifted by a wave running under it just as he was about to readjust the outboard motor, he fell in the water, and now he was swimming hard, while the inflatable was still under way, no longer steering a straight course but moving in circles, some wide, some narrower. In his attempt to grab the ring-shaped line of the inflatable, he was in danger of being forced underwater. When that happened he dived and moved aside. Sometimes I thought the boat was deliberately hunting him down. When that happened he got out of the way with a few hasty strokes.

Sudden gusts of wind showed that the weather was deteriorating. One of the first fishing cutters coming back from sea turned, got Frederik on board, and took the inflatable in tow. All the cutters were making for the safety of harbour. The spectators on the bridge dispersed as well, waiters were salvaging sun umbrellas and tablecloths and festoons from the garden café of the Seaview Hotel, and two ocean-going cutters that had been fishing for cod out at sea came into harbour as well. Long waves came rolling in, rising in the air as if a hand were pulling them up, before showing their full force as they fell and broke. Dark, ragged clouds were driving low in the sky. Suddenly I saw it, I suddenly saw the two-master outside the harbour making for our bay, coming in at a steady speed in a stiff nor'easter. Although I couldn't read the name of the yacht, I knew at once she was the *Pole Star* bringing Stella home, bringing her back to me. Then a gust struck her a visible blow, and she ran fast before the wind for a moment with all sail set. She was certainly hoping to come into harbour. I jumped off the bridge, down to the beach, and then ran to the pier. People were standing there too, watching the cutters coming home. Among them was old Tordsen, by tacit consent regarded as our harbour-master, although he had not actually been appointed or chosen for the post. Tordsen the harbour-master had eyes only for the yacht. He knew exactly what the crew were trying to do. As if issuing instructions, he muttered words of advice or warning to himself in an undertone. "Take the mainsail in, bring her in on the engine, leave the jib hoisted, just the jib, stay out there and drop anchor." He was speaking into the wind, cursing now and then, groaning as he followed every phase of the manoeuvre. I was standing right behind him, I sensed a rising fear in me, and with the fear an unfamiliar pain. I couldn't make out who was at the helm of the *Pole Star*, but there were several figures to be seen on deck. Once the yacht threatened to capsize, but a strong gust of wind brought her back on course, and it looked as if she might yet reach harbour at breakneck speed, but suddenly she reared up from the water just where we had sunk our last cargo of rocks, and an unexpected force thrust her on over the obstacle she had struck.

"Idiots!" shouted Tordsen. "You idiots!" But all he and the rest of us could do was watch the bows as they dipped under water and were thrown straight up again. They seemed to shake for a moment, and then the yacht keeled over at an angle and raced towards the wall of the harbour entrance. Her bows were forced up once more and crashed into the stone wall. The foremast broke and fell on deck, moving sideways and sweeping two of the figures on deck overboard into the crevice between the harbour wall and the hull of the boat.

"They'll be crushed!" cried Tordsen. "Get moving, Christian," he told me, "fend her off, help them to fend her off."

The three of us hung on to the side of the vessel and tried to keep her away from the stone wall as she rose and fell, but we couldn't keep the side from scraping against the stone as it made abrupt contact. The bows rose again with a grating sound, and when the crevice widened for a moment I saw two limp bodies spinning in the water below me. Climbing down to them was risky. Tordsen waved to a fishing cutter to come up, the fisherman handed us a rope with an iron hook on it – the hook he used for bringing up fish-traps that had come adrift – and we carefully set to work with it.

First we got the hook into a young man's anorak, hauled him up on deck, laid him down, and someone started working on him, pressing up and down on his chest. I wouldn't let them bring up the second body with the hook; I had recognized Stella at once, her mouth open in pain, her hair drifting over her forehead, her arms hanging powerless. I got them to make me fast and let myself down into the crevice, fending myself off with my legs. Bending low, I grabbed at empty air a couple of times, but finally I seized hold of her wrist, reached for her and got my arms under her, and at a sign from me they hauled us both up.

How you lay there on deck, Stella, motionless, arms together. I couldn't tell whether you were still breathing. I saw that you were bleeding from a head injury.

I wanted to stroke her face, but at the same time I felt a strange reluctance to touch her, I don't know why. Perhaps because I didn't want any witnesses to the intimacy of my caress. That reluctance didn't last for long. When Tordsen told the fisherman to call an ambulance to the pier at once, I knelt down beside Stella, folded her hands over her breast, and pressed and pumped as I'd seen it done in first aid so often, until water came out of her mouth first in a little stream, then in weaker jets. Her eyes were closed. "Look at me, Stella," I said, and now I did stroke her face and repeated my plea. "Look at me, Stella." She opened her eyes, an uncomprehending gaze from very far away rested on me, I went on stroking her, slowly her expression changed, there was something seeking, questioning in it, she was surely searching for something in the depths of her memory. "Christian." When her lips moved, I thought she spoke my name, but I wasn't sure. All the same I said, "Yes, Stella," and then I said, "I'll get you to a safe place somewhere."

The two men from the ambulance came along the pier with a stretcher, but once on the yacht they changed their minds. They spread a green tarpaulin on deck, carefully laid Stella on its hard canvas so that her body was entirely enclosed when they lifted her, and then, with a nod to each other, the paramedics by common consent took their burden off the yacht. Stella's body swayed slightly as they walked; it was hard for me to bear the sight. I suddenly felt as if I were lying in that tarpaulin myself. They put their burden down beside the ambulance, brought the stretcher up and laid Stella on it, and when they had fastened the safety straps they pushed the stretcher into the vehicle and the rack specially made to hold it. Without asking permission, I sat down on the folding seat next to the rack. One of the men wanted to know if I was related to her. "Family member?" was all he asked, and I said, "Yes," so he left me sitting there very close to Stella's face, which had now assumed an expression of complete indifference, or maybe resignation. During the drive we kept looking at each other, we didn't say anything, we made no attempt to speak, one of the men phoned reception at the hospital and said we were on our way. We found that we were expected outside the roofed entrance to the reception area, a young doctor took over, he spoke briefly to the two paramedics and sent me off to an office, where an elderly nurse looked up only fleetingly from her notepad. As she wrote, she too asked, "Family member?" and I said, "She's my teacher." That seemed to surprise her. She turned to me and looked at me with curiosity. I suppose she hadn't been prepared for such an answer.

It wasn't my idea to visit Stella in hospital. Georg Bisanz suggested it to me at the end of the day's lessons. He knew the visiting times; he'd been to the hospital several times to see his grandmother who, he said, had to learn to walk for the second time and was waiting for her hair to grow again.

We set off, four of us, and when the elderly nurse discovered that we wanted to visit our teacher she smiled at us and told us the floor and the room number. "You know your way around here," she said to Georg. Stella was in a room by herself. We went in quietly and slowly approached her bed. The others let me go first; an observer might have thought they were trying to keep in cover behind me. As we came in, Stella turned her head. At first she didn't seem to know who we were. No pleasure or surprise or even bafflement showed on her face, she just stared and stared, and only when I went right up to her and took her hand, which was lying on the covers, did she raise her eyes and look at me in amazement. I thought she whispered my name. Georg Bisanz was the first of us to pull himself together. He felt a need to say something, and looking down at Stella he said, "Dear Frau Petersen," and then fell silent – as if he had just taken the first hurdle. Then, after a moment, he went on. "We heard about your accident, dear Frau Petersen, and we've come to give you our good wishes. And we known you like candied fruits, so we've brought you some of your favourite nibbles" – that was what he actually said, "favourite nibbles" – "instead of flowers. They're from all of us."

Stella didn't react to what he said, not even with her familiar understanding smile. Little Hans Hansen, who wore short trousers and striped socks even in winter, thought it was up to him to say something as well, and very solemnly he offered to help her if she needed any help. Stella had only to say what he could do for her, said Hans, "just a word, Frau Petersen, and it will all be done." Stella didn't react to this offer either; she lay there looking abstracted, deep in thought, and I sensed that even I wouldn't be able to get through to her, at least not as long as the others were present. I wanted to be alone with her more and more urgently, more and more strongly.

I don't know what made Georg Bisanz think of singing Stella something, her favourite song , the one she had taught us, *The Miller of Dee*. But anyway, Georg started singing and we all joined in, suddenly finding ourselves back in the classroom with Stella standing in front of us, cheerfully conducting, encouraging us to try our voices out. We sang in loud and probably fervent tones. It was the only song we knew in English; she had sung it to us herself several times. Per Fabricius liked her voice so much that he wanted her to sing us other songs, including modern hits, he thought *I've got you under my skin* would be a good one. While we were singing we looked at her, hoping to see some kind of response, but her face gave nothing away, and I was trying to get used to her inaccessibility when something happened to make me happy. Tears appeared on your face, Stella. She didn't move her lips, she didn't raise her hand, but tears suddenly appeared on her face. They came when we reached the bit where the self-satisfied miller says, "I care for nobody, no, not I / And nobody cares for me."

Perhaps because he had heard our singing, the young doctor who had met us when Stella was brought to reception came in; he nodded briefly to us and bent over Stella, put two fingers on her throat, and then said to us, "I'll ask you young gentlemen to let my patient rest. Rest is what she needs." That was all, he said no more, although I think some of us may have hoped he would. We moved away, and as the door opened we had a brief glimpse of Georg Bisanz saying hello to his grandmother and talking to her for a moment, cheerfully and encouragingly, the way you talk to old people.

I left my classmates; I didn't go home, I went a long way round back to the hospital and sat on one of the benches donated by former patients, immortalizing them with nameplates. I sat on the bench donated by Ruprecht Wildgans and waited. I was waiting for the young doctor. I wanted to find out the most important facts about Stella from him. Visiting time was coming to an end; it was interesting to see the people coming through the swing doors, still showing how they felt about seeing their relations. Instinctively I imagined what they had seen, what they had found out, that old lady with the hard, reserved face, the elegantly dressed young woman holding hands with a little girl who was all dolled up, but began hopping and skipping as soon as she was out in the road, the young man in a hurry running to the car park, the large and obviously Turkish family – I thought I saw three generations of them – weighed down with baskets and bags. A naval officer marched smartly out through the swing doors too. The doctor I was waiting for didn't appear. I'd had practice in waiting. Nothing showed at the window of Stella's room. I thought of a wedding, the first time I'd been to one was when Aunt Trude, my mother's younger sister, married the owner of a fast-food kiosk who made his living by selling sandwiches and sausages and refreshing drinks, and my father, at the bridal couple's request, made a speech at the reception. What he said culminated in something that he meant as good advice: "If two people want to live together, they have to agree from the first over who cleans the house and who does the cooking." I couldn't get my head around the idea that this could also apply to Stella and me.

Two nurses came through the swing doors in their uniforms, followed by an old man who filled his pipe as soon as he was out in the fresh air and lit it, hastily, like an addict. He puffed hard at the pipe, looked around, and made for me. With a gesture, he asked if he could sit down beside me; in an undertone he read the name of Ruprecht Wildgans aloud, shrugged his shoulders as if to say, "Well, why not?" and then sat down. He showed me the pipe. "They won't let you smoke in there."

"I know," I said. "I know."

There was something challenging in the way he looked at me. He seemed to be wondering whether I was someone suitable for a conversation with him on this bench, and I couldn't help noticing that he was under pressure and wanted to get something off his chest. Asking no questions himself, and without any introduction, he said abruptly, "They don't know whether my son will pull through, they can't be sure, that's what his doctor said just now."

"Is he sick?"

"Sick?" he repeated, and the way he said the word sounded as if he were thinking the matter over. "Well, you could say he's sick. Sick in the head, I'd call it." He drew on his pipe and groaned, in bitterness, in despair, and referring to the misfortune that made him talkative, he said, "He tried to do away with himself."

I didn't understand what he meant at first, but after thinking for a moment he explained further. "We'll never understand how he could have done it, he shot himself in the chest, wanted to hit his heart, but he just missed it." The old man shook his head as if warding off what he was thinking now, he bit his lips, hesitated, but then went on. His misfortune seemed to force him to talk. He couldn't grasp the fact, he said, that anyone would try to kill himself these days because he hadn't passed his exam, a gifted, popular boy who knew, or ought to have known, how much had been done for his future. "Two hundred years ago, maybe, but these days?" To take his mind off it, he turned to me and assumed the right – a justifiable right – to question me, he wanted to know what brought me here. "How about you? Is one of your family in there?"

"My teacher," I said, adding, "Some of the others in my class and I went to visit our teacher. She had a bad accident."

"A car crash?"

"No, in the harbour," I said. "In a storm. She was thrown against the pier."

He thought about that, perhaps trying to work out just what had happened, and said, "Our teachers, ah, yes," and then, "I expect you think highly of her?"

"More than highly," I said, whereupon he looked at me thoughtfully, but seemed satisfied with my answer.

I guessed why he suddenly left me without a word of thanks or farewell when he made for the two men in white coats who had just come through the swing doors. They were walking towards a plain annexe building, and were deep in conversation. He shuffled after them, certainly intending to ask for confirmation of his hopes. The doctor I was waiting for myself still didn't appear. I've had practice in waiting.

As the contents of my cigarette packet shrank I thought of Stella. It was clear to me that at school we'd have to wait some time for her. They had found a substitute for Stella already, for the first lesson, an Englishman on practical teaching experience at Lessing High School. His name in itself aroused lively interest in the class; this substitute teacher was called Harold Fitzgibbon. He was not slender, not one of those tough, wiry Englishmen you get to admire in many TV films; Mr Fitzgibbon was chubby, with short, sturdy legs, and his red-cheeked face invited you to trust him. We were all pleased to hear him say good morning in English, and I was silently grateful to him for mentioning Frau Petersen's accident – "her sad misfortune" – at the beginning of the lesson, and saying he hoped she would recover soon. Familiar with the exercises that Stella had set us in her last English lessons, he praised Orwell's *Animal Farm*, and told us that at first no publisher had been prepared to bring it out, but then it was published by the firm of Warburg and became a huge success. Mr Fitzgibbon said how good your choice of a book for us was, Stella, and I couldn't help thinking he was congratulating us on having you as a teacher.

I was surprised when he wanted us to tell him what we knew about England. Stella had pointed out to us that the Germans were particularly anxious to find out what people thought about *their* country, whereas we'd wait in vain for any English person to ask, "How do you like my country?" But anyway, our temporary teacher did ask that question – we never found out how he assessed our general knowledge of England, but what he heard will certainly have given him plenty to think about. I still remember his surprise, his slight smile, his approval when we replied to his question: "What do you know about England?" An ancient kingdom, Manchester United, Lord Nelson and the Battle of Trafalgar, the mother of democracy, a passion for betting, the Whigs and the Tories, judges wearing wigs, gardens – and Peter Paustian went on enumerating gardens, having been to the British Isles once with his parents – and in addition a sense of fair play and colonies that had now been given up. Georg Bisanz seemed to have been listening to all this indifferently, unwilling to take part in the question-and-answer game, but then he suddenly said, in his usual firm voice, "Shakespeare." Mr Fitzgibbon paused in his walk up and down the room past the tables, looked at Georg and said, "Yes, indeed, Shakespeare is the greatest writer we have, perhaps the greatest in the world."

During break he was our sole subject of conversation. We talked about his looks, the way he spoke – his English accent when he talked in German was easy to imitate, and several of us had a go. A good many people wanted to have him as their teacher for the next English lesson too. I suppose no one thought then that you would never come back to our classroom.

Georg Bisanz, who had lavish supplies of pocket money – he must have got some from his grandmother – could afford more than the rest of us. That Sunday he was sitting alone at one of the wooden tables outside the kiosk. He had ordered meatballs and fruit juice, and when he saw me he invited me to come and share his snack, as he called it. Not only that: he had something to tell me, he said. He had been to the hospital, and after the usual short visit to his grandmother he decided to look in and see Frau Petersen. There was a notice on the door of her room saying, "Please do not enter Room 102 without permission." Georg did not comply with the notice; he opened the door of Stella's room and stood there in the doorway. "She was dead, Christian, she was lying there with her mouth open and her eyes closed. No doubt about it, if you ask me. She's dead."

I couldn't listen to him any longer. I set out at once, hitched a lift part of the way, went on and on, wouldn't let anyone stop me, not even the hospital porter who came out of his glazed lodge and shouted after me, or the ward nurse who signalled to me not to go any further. I knew Stella's room number, even at that moment I could rely on my memory. I opened the door without knocking.

The bed was empty, the mattress and bedspread and pillows were lying on the floor, and there was an empty vase on the bedside table. The chair for visitors still stood beside the bed, just as if it was waiting for me. I sat down beside the bed and wept, I hardly realized that I was shedding tears, at least not to start with. I became aware of it only when the tears fell on my hand and my face began burning. I didn't notice the ward nurse coming in, and she must have been standing behind me for a while before she laid a hand on my shoulder – ah, that hand on my shoulder. She didn't sound angry with me, asked no questions, didn't want to know why I was there, she let me go on weeping out of sympathy, or because her experience told her that there was nothing else to be done at such a moment. When she did speak, it was quietly, considerately. She said, "Our patient died. She's already been taken downstairs." As I said nothing, she added, "And who knows what she may have been spared? She had very severe injuries. She was flung right against the stone wall of the pier." With a consoling gesture, she left me alone.

Looking at that empty vase, I thought of Stella's father. I seemed to see him before me, sitting among his sunflowers in the little garden, and I decided to take him the news myself. At the same time I felt that I had to be where Stella had lived.

He knew already, he didn't seem very surprised to see me there in front of him. "Come in," he murmured, and went on changing his clothes, not bothered to have me watching him – just as it didn't bother my father if anyone was there when he was dressing or changing. Stella's father took my hand for a moment and pointed to the bottle of rum, showing no interest in whether I helped myself or not. Once he had put on the trousers of his dark suit – close-fitting, old-fashioned drainpipe trousers – he held the jacket up to the light, and buffed and rubbed it a little before putting it on. Perhaps I didn't hear him properly, but when he said something at last, it seemed to be "My little squirrel" – obviously he had called Stella his little squirrel when they were alone together. He disappeared into Stella's room for a while, opened drawers there, looked through school exercise books, and when he came back he gave me a letter. I recognized Stella's handwriting on the envelope. He apologized for not giving me the letter before; his daughter, he said – the old radio operator was calling her just "my daughter" now – had sent it while she was away, asking him to deliver it personally if possible. Then he apologized again and said he was going to the hospital now; they had asked him to come.

I didn't read your letter in front of him, or in

the garden or in the road. I knew it was your very last letter, so I had to read it alone in my room at home. Through the envelope, I could feel that there was a postcard inside. It was a photograph of a view, inviting people to visit a Museum of Oceanography, and showed a dolphin leaping into the air, evidently planning to come down on top of a wave. There was just a single sentence written in English on the blank side of the card: "Love, Christian, is a warm wave bearing us up," and then there was her signature, Stella. I put the postcard beside our picture, propped against my English grammar book, and felt an instinctive pang at the idea that I had missed something, or had been cheated of something, that I had wanted more than anything else in the world.

I often repeated that sentence. I felt that it was a confession, a promise, and an answer to the question that I had thought of asking, but never did.

I repeated it as I looked at our photograph, and that evening as well, when a sharp shower of rain pattered against my window, a dry pattering, rain that wasn't rain: Georg Bisanz was standing outside, picking up another handful of sand to throw it against my window pane. As soon as he saw me standing there he pointed to himself and me, and I signed to him to come up. Georg, her favourite student. He didn't stop to look around and see what my room was like, as before he felt he had to tell me what he had just found out, and it concerned me in particular. Since it was his job to carry the exercise books home for Stella, he knew her father. Georg had met him down by the navigation marks, he said, and they didn't say much to each other, but now he knew that Stella was going to be buried at sea. The two of them, the old radio operator and his daughter, had discussed all such things with each other long ago, and they both wanted to be buried at sea when their time came. So now that was to be her funeral. "Will you be coming?" he asked.

"Yes," I said.

The undertakers who arranged burials at sea had their place down by the little river mouth, a plain, windowless brick building where they worked, father and son, wearing black even in the mornings, with expressions of professional sympathy on their faces. Yes, they could tell us at once when Frau Petersen's funeral was to be. They waddled as they moved, and I couldn't help it, but they looked to me like two penguins. She was to be laid to rest on Friday morning. When I said, rather too quickly, that I wasn't a family member, one of the penguins explained, with impeccable regret, that the boat would hold only a limited number of mourners, it was a shallow vessel, a converted landing-craft, and as a great many mourners had already applied – "applied" was the word he used – including the entire school staff, they were fully booked. That was how he put it: "fully booked".

There was only a slight wind that Friday. The sky was covered with cloud, the waterfowl had left, a sense of its old indifference, so it seemed to me, lay above the bleak expanse of water. With my father's permission, Frederik and I took our tug. Frederik steered the *Endurance*, careful to keep at a distance, never crossing the course of the other vessel, and throttling back the engine we followed the former landing-craft to the place where she was to be buried, across from Bird Island. I don't know who had decided just where it would be; when we had reached the place the undertakers' boat was slackening speed, and Frederik stopped too. Both craft were rolling gently in the slate-grey sea, too far apart for any sound to carry. "Take the field-glasses," said Frederik. Through the clear lenses, I saw our principal, recognized several of my teachers, and the old radio operator. There were two wreaths lying on deck, a few bunches of flowers, and an urn standing in the middle of the flowers. Beside it, on a canvas chair, sat a stout pastor. The pastor smoothly rose to his feet and stood there firmly; he spread out his arms, obviously pronouncing a blessing first, and then, speaking with his eyes on the urn – I suppose he was turning directly to you, Stella – giving what must have been an abbreviated version of some event in your life, nodding at several sentences, just as if he didn't want anyone to doubt what he said, and I was not the only one to expect him to turn to your father, as he finally did. Then the men took off their hats, and they all took and held each other's hands. Their shoulders slumped slightly. I saw that our art teacher was weeping. The lenses were clouding over. I was shaking, and had to hold tight to the rail. I felt that our tug was beginning to heel over. Frederik must have been watching me, because he said, sounding concerned, "Sit down, boy." He left me the field-glasses.

How carefully the old radio operator picked up the urn, holding it close. He carried it to the stern of the vessel, and there, at a sign from the pastor, he opened it and held it out over the water. I had to keep thinking, Stella, that it was just a thin trail of ashes I saw coming out of the urn, drifting in the air for a moment and then dropping to the water. The sea quickly absorbed the ashes, leaving no trace behind, nothing to show they had ever been there. I could guess only at a silent disappearance, the grammar of farewell. Although your father stood there and stood there, staring at the water, there was nothing even he could do but pick up one of the wreaths. He didn't just drop it into the water, he flung it far out to sea with surprising force. After him, other people picked up the flowers and threw them into the water. Most of the flowers were tied together, but our sports teacher and two more of the staff untied the bunches and let the flowers drop singly overboard, where a very light current caught them, and it seemed to me as if they were shining as they rocked on the rippling water. At that moment I knew that those drifting flowers would be a part of my unhappiness for ever, and I would never be able to forget the consolation they offered as they illustrated my loss.

There was no doubt of it: the flowers were drifting towards Bird Island. Soon they would be cast up there, on the beach that so few people ever visited. I'll collect you, I thought, I'll come here on my own and keep you from rotting away like seaweed torn loose by rough seas, I'll put the flowers in the bird warden's hut and lay them out there to dry, they'll always be there in that place, a place that knew us, it will all be there and stay there. I'll go there in the holidays and sleep on the seagrass mattress. In my sleep we'll come close to each other, Stella, your breasts will touch my back, I'll turn to you and caress you, everything I've stored in my memory will come back again. What's past did happen, all the same, and it will last, and in the company of pain and the sorrow that goes with it, I'll try to find what can never be brought back.

When the craft carrying the mourners got under way, coming very slowly in to the bridge outside the Seaview Hotel, I asked Frederik not to follow it just yet but to go once around Bird Island. He looked at me in surprise, but then he did as I had asked him.

I looked, but I didn't really see anything that came within my field of vision. I saw Stella sitting on the tree trunk that had been washed up, sitting there in her green swimsuit, smoking, and looking as if something amused her, maybe the way I waded towards her through the waist-high water. Less certain of myself now, I gave the figure of the sitting woman your face, Stella, and while the *Endurance* rounded Bird Island a little way from the shore, I imagined that we were walking along the beach and under the alders hand in hand, and suddenly became aware that we both had secret rights of ownership here. I wasn't interested in what Frederik thought. Once past the little promontory where there were only a few birds quarrelling now – that eternal quarrel of theirs, beaks open, wings spread – Frederik asked me if I wanted to go ashore. I dismissed the idea with a gesture, and told him he could go home now, following the other boat with the mourners. Their landing-craft was already made fast to the bridge outside the Seaview Hotel, and I saw through the field-glasses that they had disembarked and were sitting at tables in the garden café.

Life – in the nature of the place, life obviously reigned here. Waiters were carrying out food and drink to the tables, mainly beer and sausages and meatballs with potato salad, and fruit tarts were also being ordered. I found a place to sit at a round table which was already occupied by Herr Kugler the art teacher, with Tordsen the harbour-master beside him. I said hello to Hans Hansen, from my class, and nodded to someone I didn't know, a round-headed man. His name was Püschkereit, he was a former staff member who had retired years ago, but he still kept in close touch with the school. He had taught history. I discovered that this Püschkereit came from Masuria in East Prussia. As soon as he said anything people began smiling, and I couldn't help smiling myself, because he used diminutives or pet words for everything. While silence weighed down on the other tables, and people exchanged glances full of meaning to suit the occasion, Püschkereit thought he ought to tell the story of a funeral in his own family, the funeral of his grandfather, who lived and died happy in a modest little house. After the meal everyone who was able and willing to tell anecdotes about the life of the deceased spoke of his kindness, his obstinacy, his friendly cunning, but also his good heart and his sense of humour. After that, when the memory of the dead grandfather had been recalled at such length that he seemed to be there among the mourners – many of the anecdotes were addressed directly to the coffin standing there in the parlour – a hired musician appeared and played music on his accordion for dancing. The harbour-master, obviously used to thinking in terms of space, wondered whether there was any room for dancing, to which Püschkereit said, "Oh yes, once we'd stood the coffin up on end there was plenty of room." He had taught history before my time. I am sure that the old radio operator, sitting at the next table, had been listening too and disapproved of this account. He rose, asked for attention, and said calmly, "No speeches, please, no speech-making here."

It didn't escape my attention that Herr Kugler was suddenly looking closely at me, frankly and as if assessing me, and after a while he gestured to me to come over and sit beside him. He told me that the staff had decided to hold an hour of remembrance in Frau Petersen's honour, in the big hall next Wednesday. "Of course one of the students ought to say a few words, and you are your class delegate, Christian, so I thought of you. And I wasn't the only one to think you should do it," he said, adding that it was to be a solemn celebration. I couldn't do it, Stella, I couldn't accept his offer, because while I was thinking about what I'd be expected to do and what I could say, a memory rose in me so violently, such an overpowering memory, that I couldn't suppress it: I saw the pillow before my eyes, the territory we had found for ourselves and shared. I understood that I couldn't give anything like that away in school, because if I did I risked destroying what meant everything to me. Perhaps the source of our happiness must rest in silence for ever. No, Stella, I didn't want to speak during the hour of remembrance. Kugler said he was sorry about that, and I asked him to forgive me for backing out. And I didn't want to stay any longer among the mourners, who were eating and drinking and moving from table to table to exchange comments on what had just happened. I didn't want to stay there, I couldn't, I just wanted to be alone.

Just as the moment for me to retreat in silence seemed to have come, I heard the droning of a powerful ship's engine coming closer. It made everyone stop and listen. A speedboat came into view, one of the new craft from the nearby naval station, towing a yacht after it on a long line, a yacht with a broken mast. I wasn't surprised that one of the naval station's boats had been brought in to salvage it, the navy had done emergency service many times, standing by anyone in difficulties out at sea, and bringing home many damaged vessels. It was the *Pole Star*, as the yacht was called, and very likely they had plugged the leaks for now and were bringing her in to the little wharf beside the naval station. Tordsen thought so too. The *Pole Star* – I just wished I knew who had thought up that name. The fast little tug passed us at a leisurely pace; no one showed on board. Not the tug itself but its image will stay in my mind for ever. I guessed that at the time, and I guessed right.

I set off for home. I walked along the beach. My eyes were stinging. Empty mussel shells broke and crunched beneath my feet, no one seemed to have noticed me leaving. I was wrong. Where the old ship's boat lay keel upwards on the beach – a bleached, untarred boat – I heard a call. Herr Block, the school principal, was sitting on the boat. He was not in the garden café with the others, he had chosen this place to be alone. With a slight wave of his hand, he invited me to come and sit down with him. Herr Block, who was usually so stiff and reserved, and who had once humiliated me, wanted to speak to me. For a while we sat there together in silence, watching the tug move out into the open sea. Suddenly he turned to me, looked at me with frank goodwill, and said, "We're going to meet in the school hall, Christian, for an hour of remembrance. Several people will speak in memory of Frau Petersen."

"I know," I said. "I've just heard about it."

"You're class delegate for your year," he said. "We thought it would be a good idea if you were to say something, speaking for the students, just briefly, just paying tribute, a few words on what the loss of our very popular teacher means to you." Since I did not reply at once, he went on. "If I'm not greatly mistaken, this loss affects you very much personally."

I just nodded. I couldn't prevent the tears from coming to my eyes. He saw that without any surprise, and touched my hand, thought for a moment and then asked, "Well, what do you say, Christian?"

I could sense that my refusal would disappoint him, but all the same I said, "I can't do it."

If he had asked me why not, I couldn't have told him. At the most, I would only have been able to say it was too early, perhaps still too soon. But he appeared satisfied, and asked only, "You'll be at the hour of remembrance all the same, though, won't you?"

"Yes," I said. "Yes, I'll be there."